SPY ROMANCE COLLECTION VOLUME 1

CONNOR WHITELEY

No part of this book may be reproduced in any form or by any electronic or mechanical means. Including information storage, and retrieval systems, without written permission from the author except for the use of brief quotations in a book review.

This book is NOT legal, professional, medical, financial or any type of official advice.

Any questions about the book, rights licensing, or to contact the author, please email connorwhiteley@connorwhiteley.net

Copyright © 2023 CONNOR WHITELEY

All rights reserved.

DEDICATION
Thank you to all my readers without you I couldn't do what I love.

AUTHOR OF THE BETTIE ENGLISH PRIVATE EYE MYSTERIES

CONNOR WHITELEY

SPYING AND ROMANCING THE NIGHT AWAY

A GAY SPY ROMANTIC SUSPENSE SHORT STORY

SPYING AND ROMANCING THE NIGHT AWAY

MI6 Officer Alexander Davies, Alex for short, had always loved the more glamourous side of spying and espionage and doing whatever it took to get the information the UK Government needed to do its business, so when he was given the opportunity to go to a black tie gallery opening filled with extremists, but admittedly hot men, he didn't have an issue in going.

Alex stood in his dark blue bedroom with the cold lonely double bed perfectly made behind him, chests of drawers filled with false passports, money and more lined the edges of the room, and Alex's favourite piece of furniture in the entire world rested right next to the large floor-to-ceiling window to his left. Alex really did love his dark brown wooden wardrobe filled with fine suits, clothes and shirts that might have been expensive but he really loved the cool, luxurious feeling of the expensive fabrics against his skin.

And on the top shelf of the wardrobe, Alex loved it that he had such a great range of aftershaves, some were poisonous to certain people and some weren't, but for tonight Alex was just going to wear his favourite. A little brand he had picked up in Paris a few years ago and even though he couldn't pronounce the name at all, he had always loved its sweet aroma of oranges, grapefruits and a subtle undertone of lemon running under it all.

That had definitely attracted a boy or two.

Alex stood in front of a large square mirror that an ex-boyfriend bought him before catching Alex in too many lies, and when the person that Alex had thought was the love of his life had found out what he did for a living, he flipped and stormed out and Alex thankfully never ever saw him again.

As Alex finished tying up his bowtie and straightening out the minor creases in his black suit made from silk that completed his outfit of a black blazer, trousers and a crisp white shirt with a little black bowtie as an added bonus, he supposed that he would have preferred to be spying on Iran, North Korea or any of the normal targets that he looked at on his computer, but it was always great to get out from time to time.

Besides from the fact that he only ever seemed to meet truly hot men on missions, but they were never the sort of men that Alex wanted to date.

They were monsters after all.

Alex had even had an offer to go clubbing tonight with some work friends, but Alex just had to go to this party, identify the leader of the extremist group that was hosting the party and leave.

To normal people that probably sounded so easy, but when the entire guest list were extremists that wanted to burn out the UK for being too soft on foreigners (but this group was talking about the Welsh, Scottish and Northern Irish who were all legal citizens of the UK) that only complicated matters.

It was even worst that Alex couldn't bring a gun or any weapons whatsoever because the party's security was so tight so Alex was hardly impressed about that.

Alex finally managed to get his bowtie perfectly straight and he had to admit that he looked great in his black suit, and it was just a shame that no one attractive or into Alex in the slightest would ever see him in it.

That was definitely one of the worst things about being a spy. Alex truly adored MI6 for having enough faith in him to let him travel the world, spying on the UK's enemies and protecting the innocent people of the UK. But the only real problem was that it was so lonely at times.

MI6 hardly hired that many gay people, unlike MI5, so it was next to impossible to date and it was even harder to find gay friends that actually understood him. Sure there were some posh snobs from the English nobility that had been casted out of their rich families for being gay, but that was far from the same.

Especially as Alex had been born to a poor family, no mother and only raised by his father who had celebrated Alex when he finally came out.

So Alex hardly fitted in with the rich posh snobs of MI6 and the English "nobility".

Alex dashed out the door of his London apartment and really looked forward to travelling across London to this extremist party.

The idea of spying on a group of extremists with certain death being the consequence if he got caught excited him way more than it should have.

***

French DGSE agent Hugo Petain had never ever understood why the English were obsessed with three things, like they were the only things that mattered in the entire world, judging by the past hour of conversations Hugo had had with these extremists, it seemed the English were only concerned with burning down the three other nations of the UK because of these dirty foreigners, killing off socialism for good and most importantly, making sure the disease-ridden French stopped invading the UK.

Hugo had no idea where some of these extremists got those ideas from, but when the President of France asked Hugo specifically to come to this awful party filled with the very worst kind of English people, he supposed he had no choice.

And it was a great benefit that Hugo could

control his French accent perfectly, and it did make him very popular at French parties because Hugo could do any accent perfectly that his friends asked of him.

It was also remarkably helpful in spy work too.

After an hour of talking with so many extremists in their tight black suits, horrible oxford-laced (or whatever they were called) black shoes and black trousers, Hugo just stood at the back of the very large function room the party was in and just studied it like he had another three times tonight.

The function room itself was horrible and terribly English with its dark brown oak walls that seemed to suck out all the light of the room, there were bookcases filled with first editions built into the four walls (but Hugo seriously doubted any of these extremists could read) and there was a very large chandelier hanging from the white textured ceiling.

The chandelier itself was certainly French made judging by the craftsmanship, so Hugo was a little surprised these people wanted something so disease ridden at their party, but it just proved how stupid all these people were.

But even Hugo had to admit that he really did love the stunning skyline of London with all its skyscrapers, ancient landmarks and little lights that lit up the horizon through the massive floor-to-ceiling windows that were dotted about on the wall to Hugo's right.

Hugo had rather enjoyed tonight so far because

for the most part the English were just troublemakers, or at least their politicians were, but he had to admit the English did produce some very fine-looking men. Of course mainland European men were always more beautiful than the English, but Hugo wouldn't mind bedding some of these extremists for information purposes, of course.

Hugo leant against an icy cold oak wall nursing his small glass of whiskey from almighty Scotland, now there was a country that Hugo could fully support and move to, and it was just another sign that these extremists were hypocrites.

Hugo was really looking forward to leaving the party so he could crack on with some missions whilst he was in the UK. He did need to hack into the UK Government and see what post-Brexit rubbish they were planning so at least France could prepare defence measures, a small top-secret MI6 boat patrol had already invaded French waters and killed ten soldiers.

Including Hugo's boyfriend of five years, so he was hardly impressed with the British Secret Service and he was more than happy that the Director of DGSE had given him permission to hack into MI6 too if he wanted it.

And Hugo really did want it.

"Mr Petain," a very elderly and fragile man said in an expensive suit as he walked up to Hugo.

Hugo bowed his head slightly, because that was what apparently the English did when they met a "superior" even though surely everyone should have been equal at this party.

"We are grateful for your donation to our cause, please thank your wife for us," the man said.

Hugo raised his glass. "I will thank you dear sir. It is only because of the brave men like you and your friends that there is a chance for us to be free of the smelly French and extremist Scots, Welsh and Irish,"

"Hey, hey," the man said cheering with Hugo.

As soon as the man wandered off Hugo felt like he was going to be sick. At least the money that Hugo had transferred to this extremist group's bank account had been revealed the name all their accounts were under, and with most of them being based in the EU, the DGSE was leading the charge in freezing the accounts now.

Hugo just wanted to see who was in charge though, everyone at the party had said that the boss was turning up later to reveal the new plans for an "event" that would help them to get rid of the French once and for all, so Hugo sadly had to stay a little longer.

Hugo was about to finish his drink when he noticed a new person walk in, and Hugo straightened his back just in case this guy was the boss or something.

Wow.

Hugo just stared wide-eyed and like a deer in headlights as he watched the absolutely gorgeous sexy man walk into the party, looking a little lost.

Hugo simply loved the man's tight expensive black silk blazer, trousers and white shirt that highlighted how sensationally fit he was under all those clothes. The man was so beautiful and perfect that Hugo just didn't know what to do.

His hands turned sweaty, his heart started to beat faster and he was just so beautiful that Hugo really, really wanted to run his hands through the gorgeous man's longish well-styled brown hair.

He was beyond hot, and he was far more beautiful than any English man deserved to be.

And even though he was probably a foul awful extremist that would be serving life sentences in a few years' time Hugo just had to talk to this gorgeous man.

Just in case he wasn't.

***

Alex was immediately hit with the aromas of strong whiskey, French cheese and another strange but awful smell that he just couldn't detect yet.

Alex wasn't even a fan of the function room itself, it was very upper-class English with so much poshness and snobbiness built into the room that Alex just wanted to leave. He really didn't like the dark brown oak walls, the first-editions in the built bookcases that were rather vaguer in his opinion, but he had to admit he did like the French chandelier.

Alex could instantly tell that it was French because it was so classy, sparkling and rather dazzling in a way that English made goods were very rarely done. It really did help to bring the room together but at least Alex knew that he was dealing with hypocrites, he hated fighting hard-line true-believer extremists.

But hypocrites were a lot more manageable.

Alex started looking at all the very tall and fit extremist men in their tight black suits and horrible oxford laced shoes and their pompous attitudes that Alex didn't agree with in the slightest. And whilst Alex completely believed that the UK and Britain could become "great" again, it most certainly wasn't going to become great through extremism and killing.

Yet these people probably disagreed entirely.

"Hello," a man said. "I'm Hugo Petain,"

Alex looked around to see who was talking to him and… holy fuck.

Alex's mouth actually dropped when he saw a very cute tall guy standing next to him, offering out his hand. Alex seriously loved the man's strong jawline, short but extremely cute looking blond hair and bright sapphire eyes.

He was just so cute.

And Alex seriously loved the man in his tight black suit that left very little to the imagination, at least Alex knew that he was well-endorsed below, that was always a bonus.

Alex felt his stomach fill with butterflies and blood rushed to wayward parts as he shook the cute guy's hand, and Alex thought he was going to faint as the sheer rush of attraction, chemistry and affection flowed between them.

Then Alex wondered if the man was going to kiss his hand, like they occasionally did in France at times, but the cute guy seemed to stop himself.

When Alex's face started to hurt from smiling so much, he realised that he hadn't intended to smile at this cute guy, but he was so beautiful.

But Alex couldn't understand what a French man was doing here. Sure the man didn't look French or say it in the slightest, but if the man was a spy then it meant nothing. And Petain was definitely a French surname dating back to at least to the 40s with the head of the Vichy Government in World War two.

Alex simply smiled as the cute guy as they sadly broke their handshaking and the cute guy passed him a drink of strong Scottish whiskey, but inside Alex was a bit concerned, he had only heard last night that MI6 had illegally killed a bunch of French soldiers for no reason on the orders of the Prime Minister.

Alex and basically every single MI6 agent had been outraged but if the DGSE was running operations on British soil, then he was starting to get a little concerned about what the hell this meant for his own safety.

Alex made sure no one else was within earshot and then leant very close to the cute guy, and Alex seriously loved the amazing earth smell of the guy.

"What is the DGSE up to?" Alex asked quietly.

The cute guy laughed a little like Alex had told him a joke, he was very good.

"I presume you are MI6 then, a little odd for British murderers to be operating on UK soil," Hugo said.

Alex felt his stomach flip, clearly this Frenchman was annoyed about the murders.

"I had nothing to do with that and I *flat out* hated my government for doing it," Alex said with a lot more conviction than he intended.

Hugo raised the glass to his lips and Alex just smiled because he wasn't drinking, it only looked like he was drinking. So Alex did the same, they were at a party after all.

A very elderly man walked past and Alex pulled Hugo slightly closer to him. "Believe me if I can help the DGSE I will, I am nothing like those agents from the other night,"

Again Alex was rather surprised at his conviction and it was only now that he was realising how much he utterly hated those MI6 agents, he didn't even know why they went to France in the first place and came across those soldiers.

Hugo slowly nodded, taking another fake sip of his whiskey. "I appreciate that,"

It wasn't exactly the glowing endorsement Alex had wanted but at least Hugo sounded a lot less annoyed with him than before, and that only made him seem cuter.

"What does MI6 have on the leader of the party?" Hugo asked as he led Alex through the crowd and nodded at several extremists like they had been friends for years.

"Nothing. The same as DGSE?" Alex asked.

Hugo smiled and manly hugged a very fragile man who started muttering some slogan about how the foul Scots needed to die and then only in their ashes could England rise to true greatness.

Alex took Hugo's light laughter as a yes that the DCSE had nothing.

"Gentleman!" a young man shouted near the front of the function room and all eyes fixed on him. "Our Lord and Saviour is here to enlighten us all on the Final Order,"

Alex had no clue what the Final Order was but it hardly sounded good and as Alex's stomach flipped he had a very sudden urge to protect hot sexy Hugo no matter what.

Because no one that hot and cute and wonderful deserved to suffer.

***

Hugo had to admit that Alex was really hot and beautiful, and he had actually loved spending time with him. It was such a relief to know that he wasn't like other MI6 agents, and at least he wasn't a murderer. He was just a cute little Englishman that had the power to melt Hugo's heart and his wayward parts flare to live.

"Here is our Saviour," the young man said, who was wearing the same tight black suits as all the other men in the function rooms with its French chandelier, bookcases built into the dark brown oak walls and plenty of little pieces of food now going around on little palates. Again a French invention.

A few moments later a very tall middle-aged man stepped into the room with messy blond hair, a massive stomach and the sort of grin that Hugo just had from slimy politicians that he had or may have not assassinated in his long career.

"Saviour," the young man said bowing.

Everyone else bowed so Hugo forced himself to and gorgeous Alex followed.

"Rise," the Saviour said.

Hugo focused on the man and tried to place him in all the photos he had studied of English politicians, known extremists and nobility he had studied before the mission, but he couldn't place him. He had no clue who he was.

And judging by Alex's beautiful face, he didn't have a clue either. This was a brand new player, and that never ended well.

"We have been infiltrated by the disease-Ridden, the Corrupt MI6 and even the Conspiracy Theorist Americans that broke away from our divine Empire hundreds of years ago," the Saviour said.

Hugo looked around like everyone else did in utter horror at such an outrageous and disgusting thing, Hugo really like these parts of missions when his acting skills got put to the test.

Yet he was a bit surprised that someone from the CIA was here.

"Two nights ago," the Saviour said, "I sent a

group of Divine Heroes from MI6 into the disease-ridden land of mainland Europe,"

Everyone gasped like that was the most heroic and most unbearable thing they had ever heard. Hugo just wanted to laugh at these pathetic people who had probably never seen the beautiful landscapes of Paris, Budapest and the other wonders of ancient Europe.

It really was beautiful.

And Hugo really wanted to share some of those beautiful views with Alex. He even wondered if the beauty of those views would be amplified or diminished by Alex's own stunning beauty.

"I ordered them to attack a small DGSE outpost to stop them from developing a nuclear weapon to attack us with and when my agents were there from MI6 they hacked into their databases and learnt the identity all French agents tainting our most holy island," the Saviour said.

Hugo was just amazed that these idiots were buying it. France didn't have much of a nuclear programme these days and they most certainly didn't plan to use it against the British.

The opposite was quite the case.

Beautiful Alex took a step closer to him. "You should leave now. I don't want you to get hurt,"

Hugo was about to say a witty comeback to the insult of his honour, but then he heard the amount of emotion and interest and actual caring in his voice.

Hugo had no clue if Alex wanted to protect him so he, as a Frenchman, wouldn't die or if Alex actually cared about him romantically, but Hugo wasn't leaving.

This was his fight and he had to stay and protect Alex.

Then Hugo felt the cold metal barrel of a gun press into his back and Hugo noticed two guys were standing behind him and Alex.

"And I didn't mention Swig," the Saviour said to Hugo, "but the foul traitorous Americans have earned their redemption and a single CIA asset has joined us,"

Hugo turned around slowly and just frowned at the grey bushy beard, slim body and brown eyes filled with rage of the American holding the gun on Alex.

The two men with the guns gestured Hugo and Alex to go forward.

Hugo turned back around and slowly went forward, he almost wanted to laugh at the disgusted looks of the extremists as they realised they had actually hugged a Frenchman, and a gay one at that.

When Hugo and Alex got to the front of the function room next to a bright red row of red first-edition hardbacks, Hugo just glared at the Saviour and changed his accent back to normal.

"You know half of these idiots hugged me tonight?" Hugo said.

Saviour shrugged and looked at his audience. "The real problem with the French is that their disease corrupts their voices so you cannot understand these monsters, but I think my translation of the Creature's tongue is correct,"

Bullets screamed through the air.

Twenty extremists dropped dead as men lining the outside of the function room shot all the people had that hugged and been tainted by Hugo's so-called disease ridden touch tonight.

At least that was twenty more people they didn't need to fight.

The Saviour whipped out a gun.

Alex shot forward.

Protectively placing himself between the gun and Hugo.

That was sweet and Hugo really appreciated it but now wasn't the time for romance. Especially as Hugo just needed to touch the Saviour and his friends might turn on him.

Especially if Hugo shouted French that the extremist might take as a diseasing curse.

The CIA agent punched Alex. He fell against the first editions.

"Damn it," the Saviour said. "Add burning those hardbacks to the list. We can't have fag-contaminated stuff in our party room. We can't have the mental disorder spreading to our members,"

Hugo just laughed.

Alex smiled at him and he was so cute.

"Shall we cause some trouble?" Hugo asked gesturing towards the Saviour.

The atmosphere changed in intensity. It was so tense and all the extremists looked like they were almost too shocked that something so disgusting was in front of them that they were all too stunned to do anything about it.

Exactly how Hugo wanted them.

Alex nodded. He flew at the CIA Agent.

Hugo surged forward.

Charging at the Saviour.

He screamed in pain.

A man tackled Hugo.

Throwing him against the bookcases.

Whacking Hugo across the face.

Hugo blocked the punches.

Hugo kicked him in the balls.

The man fell to the ground.

Hugo kicked him in the head.

The Saviour was running away.

Hugo jumped through the air.

Tackling the Saviour to the ground.

The Saviour screamed.

The entire room stopped. Hugo kissed the Saviour on the lips.

It was so disgusting that Hugo just wanted to vomit so badly that when two black suited men pulled Hugo off him, and placed him in a headlock.

Hugo actually did vomit all over the carpet.

Everyone gasped as the Saviour stood up and Hugo and Alex just laughed, because the Saviour's wayward parts were very excited about the kiss to Hugo's utter dismay.

The two men released Hugo and Hugo

immediately made sure that Alex was okay and he was just standing on three corpses with broken necks like it was just another day at the office, because in a way it really was.

"Cover me," Alex said, as he carefully got his phone.

Hugo nodded.

"You are a fag traitor," all the extremists said as one.

"No I am pure. I am straight. I am divine," the Saviour pleaded.

All the extremists took out small pocket knives and the CIA agent punched the Saviour in the face before putting him in a headlock.

"Let's show this fag what we do to them," the CIA agent said.

Hugo watched all the foul extremists as they lined up and sliced the Saviour's flesh through his expensive suit.

Hugo quickly realised that they were going to kill by death by a thousand cuts, an extremely painful way to go but the Saviour deserved it.

"A strike team will be here in minutes," Alex said as he took Hugo's hands. "You have to go now,"

Hugo just looked at gorgeous the Englishman in front of him. A man that was so beautiful that Hugo really didn't want to leave him, because for the first time in ages, he actually felt great, alive and like there was fun in his work once more.

Three feelings he hadn't realised he had missed in

spy work for a long, long time.

But he knew that Alex was right, if the strike team caught him then he would be turned over to MI6 and then the politicians would get involved with news of such a priced French asset in their custody.

Hugo would just be used by the English in their constant pointless fighting with mainland Europe, and chances are Hugo would never be freed because the English would keep changing their demands like they always did.

"Please," Alex said.

Bullets screamed through the air.

Hugo threw Alex to one side.

Bullets slammed into the bookcase behind them.

The men charged at Hugo.

Hugo punched a man.

Three men grabbed Alex.

Alex couldn't fight them off.

Hugo kicked the men in the heads.

Snapping a neck.

A knife zoomed past Hugo's head.

He caught the arm connected to it.

Slamming the arm over his knees.

Shattering bone.

Doors downstairs exploded open.

People stormed in.

Automatic rifles fired.

Corpses tumbled downstairs. The Strike team was here.

The CIA man kicked Hugo in-between the legs.

He collapsed to the ground.

The CIA man stuck a gun in Hugo's mouth.

Hugo jumped forward.

Surprising the man.

Hugo broke the man's arm.

He dropped the gun.

Hugo grabbed the gun.

Shooting the CIA man in the head.

His brain matter exploded out.

The strike team breached the room.

Hugo had to go. He had to leave beautiful Alex.

Hugo ran towards a floor-to-ceiling window.

Shot at it.

The window shattered.

Hugo grabbed a long curtain next to it.

And jumped out the window.

***

Alex was amazed as sexy cute Hugo leapt out the window, snapping the curtain rail off the wall but because the curtain rail was so long it didn't fall out the window, effectively breaking Hugo's fall.

Alex carefully went over to the window and stared down at the little balcony below that was only a few metres above the street level, an easy jump for a spy to make, and Hugo simply waved at Alex and blew him a kiss before he disappeared into the night.

And it was exactly then Alex felt absolutely awful, because it had been so much fun working and spying alongside Hugo. Alex had felt alive, young and it was the most fun he had had in ages.

As Alex watched the shadow of Hugo disappear into the night and darkness of London, he just felt so alone again. Because Alex was only realising now how much it had meant to him that he had actually got the chance to meet another gay spy, and a really, really cute one at that.

"Agent Davis," a man said behind Alex.

Alex turned around and smiled as he saw his boss Mr Blake Evans, well the person in charge of his department anyway not the head of MI6, a middle-aged man with a bald head wearing jeans, a t-shirt and some black shoes that made Alex instantly know that his boss had come here to make sure *he* was okay, and not on some official MI6 business.

As the extremists cursed and swore their revenge on the disease-ridden French and the fag English that were burning this country to the ground, Alex just laughed and when the strike and everyone had left, leaving just Alex and his boss in the function room until MI6's crime scene techs came, he just noticed that Blake was grinning at him.

"I heard Hugo Petain was in the country," his boss said. "A very cute and attractive *gay* French DGSE agent,"

Alex shook his head. "Sounds like a great guy, a real ally to this country. I hope I get to meet him one day,"

Blake laughed. "Come on Alex, you know I have power with the Head of the Agency,"

Alex shrugged again pretending to act cool, but

he was surprised when Blake took a step closer.

"And in confidence, I can tell you both the UK and French Governments want more collaboration so they want two agents working together constantly, if you catch my drift,"

Alex smiled, not because the UK government actually wanted collaboration with the French, but because that might mean him and cute Hugo could be spending a lot more time together. Of course he just couldn't admit that Hugo was here tonight just because in case some idiot wanted to moan at the French for running ops on UK soil without permission.

Like the UK or any country was any better.

Alex smiled and shrugged as he walked out the function room. "If you did recommend me for it I wouldn't object it too, I have never met this cute Frenchman you're talking about but I would like to,"

Blake just laughed, and Alex was really, really excited about getting the amazing chance to work alongside with such a cute, beautiful Frenchman like Hugo.

He actually couldn't wait because he just had a feeling that he was deadly sure about would only be confirmed with a couple of dates and then even more all over the world, that the feelings of attraction, affection and chemistry was never going to fade between him and Hugo.

And what they had both personally and professionally felt was going to be amazing, fun and definitely last until death til them part.

***

Two years later Hugo leant against the wonderfully warm marble railing of their hotel balcony overlooking the stunning, magical and beautiful city of Paris with his brand new husband Alex leaning against him. Hugo had always known it was going to be magical working alongside with such a gorgeous man but it had been so much more than he ever could have imagined.

Together Hugo and Alex had taken down terror groups in the middle east, stopped the assassination of the French President (many times) and saved more European leaders than either one of them cared to think about, and whilst Hugo and Alex were heroes throughout France and European in the intelligence community, back in the UK Alex barely got mentioned in any praise. Not that either of them really cared anymore.

With the fiery bright red, orange and yellow sun starting to set behind the stunning Eiffel Tower and casting long shadows on the little narrow streets of Paris filled with bakeries, pastries and so many more wonders that Hugo just looked forward to exploring with his beautiful husband, Hugo really did feel at peace.

The air was so crisp and warm and filled with delightful aromas of pastries that Hugo never wanted to leave this stunning city again, but as he looked at the beautiful man that was his stunning husband,

Hugo realised that he didn't need a place to feel at moment or at home.

He only needed Alex.

So as the sun continued to set and Hugo just held Alex in his arms, really enjoying the feel of Alex's fine expensive suit against his firm body, Hugo was of course really looking forward to their honeymoon in his home-city of Paris, but he was more than looking forward to getting back out into the world and seeing what spy missions they had to do.

There were a lot of threats in the world to stop, and before he met Alex, that concerned, scared and even worried Hugo but now he had such a great, fun-loving and skilful partner, it was simply something to look forward to.

Because they were together, and that's exactly what made them unstoppable.

Alex turned around in Hugo's arms and pulled Hugo closer, kissed him and smiled.

"Have you ever had sex with a married Englishman?" Alex asked seductively.

"I've had sex with lots of married people as a spy. Men and women, but never an English one, why?" Hugo asked, his smile only growing more and more.

Alex moved his hands slowly down Hugo's body and came so close to his ear that Hugo could feel his wonderful warm breath on his ear.

"Because when English people get married we get a lot hungrier for romance," Alex said kissing

Hugo on the neck.

"You clearly haven't met French people before when they get married," Hugo said, grabbing both of Alex's hands and pulling him back into their hotel room for a very romantic night of international love that would certainly last the whole night.

But Hugo just knew that their love would last, a very, very long time indeed.

LOVE, SPIES AND RHINELAND
8th March 1936
Paris, France

Amateur Spy Alice Foutain stood on her little black balcony overlooking the amazing city of Paris. She seriously loved this wonderful city with its immensely tall (at least to her) apartment blocks that seemed to simply grow out of the ground, the little bakeries and shops that popped up on every street corner and the delightful spirit of her fellow French citizens.

Alice had moved to Paris soon after the end of the 1914-1918 war from England. She never had liked England too much compared to France, and even now Alice just loved staring out over the city as the sun dimly rose in the distance.

Alice liked the sensational smells of freshly baked breads, pain-au-chocolat and croissants that veiled the city every single morning. In all honesty that was the city's natural alarm clock, and Alice always made a point to leave her apartment windows open in the summer just so she could wake up to that sensational smell. Even now the outstanding taste of chocolate and fresh bread that would melt into buttery deliciousness formed on her tongue.

Alice had often wondered if she had had what it would take to become a great French chef. Back in the little village she grew up in, she was a legendary cook supplying the troops and families and children's parties with her delights and cakes.

It was actually how she had met most of her friends, but ever since moving to Paris she had just felt like such an amateur cook and amateur everything compared to the French wizards that could create anything they set their minds to.

But she did love this amazing city.

Alice was still a little surprised with herself that she had managed to take to a brand new city so quickly after the war. She had lost her husband, her family and most importantly her best friends to the barbaric Germans, so she just needed to escape into a new country.

Granted, the news of the German invasion of Rhineland yesterday had hardly seemed to affect Paris whatsoever.

Especially with all the cute Parisian men walking about casually in their black pinstripe suits with their double-breasted jackets and wide lapels, and their workman's caps on their heads. Definitely a more interesting fashion choice than England, but Alice could hardly complain too much.

Even if the workmen looked like they lived, worked and breathed in the dirty docks and factory, they still looked better than Alice in her taggy dressing gown that her mother had given her decades ago. She really did need to replace it at some point, but she had a lot more to focus on for now.

The sheer uncaring attitude towards the invasion shocked Alice more than she wanted to ever admit, France was one of the three countries that had created the Treaties of Versailles and forced the Germans to abide by the rules.

An invasion of Rhineland was in direct contrast to at least three of the articles in the Treaties. And it was just flat out ridiculous that no one seemed to care that Germany and stupid Hitler had simply broken the laws and articles of the Treaties, and no one cared.

Alice had fought in the war against the Germans relaying messages and commands through the British Empire. She knew exactly how murderous, awful and foul the Germans were but how the hell could the French not care?

Saying that she highly doubted the British were going to do anything. The British never got involved in anything these days unless it directly affected them, and Alice failed to see how a so-called little invasion was a threat to the even more so-called might of the British Empire.

More and more gentle hints of freshly baked breads, pastries and other wonders tried to infiltrate Alice's senses, almost like they wanted to relax her, but she wasn't having it.

If France and other countries were going to let Hitler destroy international law and increase their military to a concerning size, then she was going to prepare herself and her friends. That was one of the good things about being a former soldier and serving in France during the 1914-18 war, she was still invited to all the French military parties with all the top commanders and their friends.

Alice just smiled at meeting the wonderful Mary-

Madeline and her like-minded friends were who just as concerned about the rising influence of Hitler, the Treaties and the "Nazi" movement (whatever that was). Alice really hadn't been expecting to get a call from her late last night about meeting at a local café, so Alice went along, if anything else to just see a friendly face at the end of a chaotic day.

Alice flat out hadn't been expecting to get covertly recruited to be a contact for Mary-Madeline and the informant network she was hoping to build across France, Germany and Switzerland. But Mary-Madeline had put it so perfectly, Alice had friends in the French military and she had a way with people that would make them tell her things.

Mary-Madeline was hardly wrong about that, Alice loved getting close to people and getting them to tell her their secrets. It was how she got a British Commander who was copping too many feels for her liking to back the hell off. Secrets and information and knowledge were currency in this day and age.

Alice was no fool about that.

Alice checked the little rusty watch on her wrist and rolled her eyes at the ungodly time it was. It was approaching nine o'clock in the morning and she was meant to be meeting a friend of Mary-Madeline to try and recruit him.

Alice could hardly say she was too impressed about it all, considering she knew nothing about him except a general description and that he was a truck driver who frequently drove in and out of Germany's industrial regions. So he was definitely the sort of informant Alice wanted in the network if what she feared was true.

Because as everyone Alice had spoken to since

the invasion of Rhineland had said, it isn't a question of if Hitler will attack more countries and break the Treaties further.

It is very much a question of when.

***

8th March 1936
Paris, France

Truck Driver Bastian Lefebvre sat in his favourite seat at the very back of a little café tucked far down into a little alley that few people went down. Bastian had always loved the café's cosiness, little round tables and constant smell of cigar smoke.

The cigar smoke also served the rather grand purpose of thinly veiling the café so it was near impossible to see from one side of the café to another. Bastian had managed to get used enough to the veil of smoke to understand if a threat had just walked into the café, that little trick had saved him a few times already.

Now he just hoped it would save him even more.

The sound of other people talking, laughing and playing cards was low and soft which Bastian really liked. The last thing he wanted for this meeting was for the man he was meeting to be put off by all the noise. He needed this meeting to go perfectly.

Bastian gently tapped his foot on the hard wooden floor of the café and just hoped this man he was meeting was going to show up soon. He just needed to become part of this network and help defeat the German invasion that was coming.

Bastian had already told his very few remaining family members about his fears, but they had just laughed at him. But they hadn't driven through Rhineland in the past few days and the other parts of

Germany. He hadn't seen so many German flags, military vehicles and troopers since the Dark Days.

A shiver ran down Bastian's spine just thinking about the Dark Days as him and his brother called them. France was hit bad enough through the 1914-1918 war, both him and his brother had fought endlessly and the days just rolled into one as the chaos and death stretched out endlessly.

Then Bastian's brother had been killed by chlorine gas and it was exactly then that Bastian had vowed never to allow such a war to happen again.

Of course Bastian had tried to sign up for any government roles that involved Germany or the Treaties of Versailles, but he was declined for all. He had tried to become a French soldier again after the war but he was declined. Bastian even tried to join the French Security Services, but they just laughed at his concerns that the war could ever happen again.

As the sound of people slurping their coffee made Bastian frown, he just hoped that they were right. And maybe they were, after all they were the intelligence services. They surely had access to all the agents, reports and other vital pieces of information on the Germans.

But what if they weren't correct?

Bastian felt his stomach tighten into a painful knot. He couldn't let France fall again, wouldn't that just be a failure to his brother and all of the amazing people that had been butchered by the Germans?

"Hello?" a woman's voice said in French from close by.

Bastian looked around and was shocked to see a woman standing right in front of him. What the hell was she doing here? He hoped she wouldn't scare off the man he was meant to be meeting. Spy work didn't have any place for women, women would just slow down the network's job.

"Excuse me, I'm waiting for someone," Bastian said.

The woman simply smiled, and Bastian had to admit she was actually stunning. Bastian loved the way she looked so sexy, alluring and seducing in her little blue flowery dress that tightly fitted her hourglass frame, and the stunning blue of the dress only amplified the shocking beauty of her eyes.

Bastian seriously wanted to talk and get to know this stunning woman, and he definitely wouldn't have minded running his fingers through her long wavy blond hair. She looked like she could be a fashion model, but then again Bastian had to get her away from him so she wouldn't scare off the man he was meant to be meeting.

The woman leant closer to Bastian. Bastian really loved the delightful hints of violets, lavenders and lilacs that came from her perfume. She smelt divine.

"Are you a friend of Mary-Madeline?" the woman asked.

Bastian just frowned. "Seriously? You're the person I'm meeting. I thought I was meeting a man. How the hell are you meant to do spy work?"

The woman simply let out a light laugh and sat down on the chair opposite him. The woman looked so amazingly hot and sexy that Bastian was actually starting to warm up to the idea of him working with her.

But if Bastian's suspicions were true, he highly doubted that a woman could be useful in the war to come.

***

8th March 1936
Paris, France

Alice was highly impressed that she hadn't punched the man right there and then. How dare he imply that women couldn't do spy work, this was exactly the sort of crap and utter bullshit she had to deal with as a messenger.

Alice would have loved to see those stupid pathetic men drive through dense forests with German squads chasing her on her motorbike in order to deliver vital intelligence to Command. She had done that. Not men.

Even this little café was a disgrace to the stunning city of Paris with its cigar smoke and sheer inelegance. She expected this sort of thing in England, not the delightfully elegant city of Paris.

"Believe me," Alice said, "I saw and did things in the war that even men couldn't do,"

Alice was really pleased with herself for keeping her tone cold, calm and deadly. She wasn't going to look silly here, she was in control and quite frankly this man needed to buck his ideas up if there was any hope of their informant network growing to actually be useful in the upcoming war.

"Alice," she said, holding out her hand.

The man smiled and hesitated. "Bastian, English?"

Alice was impressed and when Bastian shook her head she was shocked to feel butterflies fly around in her stomach, her palms turned clammy and her heart even skipped a few beats.

Then Alice really focused on the man she was talking to. He was rather attractive she supposed with his black pinstripe suit that suggested a good looking muscular figure down below, and his dark green workman's cap somehow managed to illuminate the dark green emeralds he had for eyes.

And there was just something so... handsome about him, and wonderfully manly about his strong jawline and features.

Alice wanted to roll her eyes at herself. She couldn't seriously be falling for such a horrible sexist pig, but there was just something about him.

After seducing so many men during the war when she had gotten captured and to just get intelligence when her commander needed it most, Alice had learnt when there was more to a man that he was trying to hide. And Alice couldn't deny that she just felt like there was a lot more to this man than he was letting on.

"You're a truck driver," Alice said, "who drives through Rhineland and the other parts of Germany, correct?"

Alice loved it how Bastian just couldn't look at her and had to look at the cold wooden floor. That was exactly the sort of reaction she wanted, he had clearly seen something that startled him and that was probably why Mary-Madeline had wanted him.

"What did you see?" Alice asked.

Bastian looked at her, and Alice slightly enjoyed staring into the dark emerald eyes of this attractive man.

"I don't want to burden you. You probably haven't experienced the horrors of the war, I don't wish that on anyone," he said.

Alice just smiled. She didn't know why it was so hard for men to understand that she had killed

Germans with her bare hands, escaped impossible situations and had actually been present for the signing of the Treaties of Versailles.

So she told him.

Whenever Alice told men what she had done, there was only two reactions that men had. Three-quarters of men flat out didn't believe her and firmly believed she should be in prison for lying. Then the last quarter had the exact same reaction as Bastian.

Alice's just smiled at Bastian as his eyes widened, his smile grew and he actually changed his outlook on her.

Alice had seen it all before. When she walked into most rooms men believed she was a silly little woman who couldn't be useful in the slightest, but after they learned what she had been through. They changed their tune and started seeing her as a strong peer, not a woman but an equal, because in all honesty that was exactly how she had wanted to be seen.

Because if the war had taught her anything, it was that regardless of your gender, country or beliefs when you were in the trenches they didn't matter in the slightest.

Only your abilities mattered.

And as she stared into those stunningly dark emerald eyes, Alice just knew that this was a kindred spirit who wanted to hit the Germans just as hard as she did.

***

8th March 1936

Paris, France

Bastian couldn't believe that he was sitting with such an amazing woman, and he felt incredibly guilty about thinking poorly of her earlier. But she was incredible, she had done so many things that Bastian doubted most men could actually do.

Over the course of the next few hours, Bastian and sexy Alice had drank plenty of cups of coffee, ordered a little breakfast that they shared and they had just spoken about the Dark Days.

But that was the amazing thing about Alice, she didn't see it as the Dark Days. Sure she had lost her family, husband and best friends, but she still had so much infectious hope about France and the world.

And even Bastian was starting to feel hopeful about the future all because of this sexy woman. For the first time since his brother had been gassed, Bastian actually felt alive again and able to enjoy life.

"So what happens now?" Alice asked.

The question sort of hit Bastian like a ton of bricks. Sure he had been expecting their wonderful morning to end at some point, but he didn't want it to end. He wanted to keep talking and spending time with this stunning woman.

He wanted, needed to keep listening to her plans about the future, the informant network and learning about her. She was one of the most incredible women he had ever met, he didn't want to lose her.

Bastian took her hand. Bastian really loved the wonderful softness of her little hands in his, and he enjoyed the chemistry that flowed between them.

"Will you be my handler for the network?" Bastian asked.

It was a good question, Bastian wanted any excuse to spend more time with her. If there was even a chance that the Germans and the company he worked for would accept a woman driver, then he would have absolutely asked her to join him.

But that would never happen.

Then Bastian noticed that Alice seemed tense and confused and hesitant. Had he said something wrong?

Bastian was sure that they had a good connection that they needed to explore even further. Bastian wanted to spend the rest of the day with her, and hopefully the night, Bastian just wanted to get to know this incredible woman even more.

"I don't know. I like you. But…" Alice said.

Bastian slowly shook his head. He should have twigged it sooner when Alice had been talking about her husband. She had been conflicted about starting or wanting to start a new relationship.

Like so many since the day of the war, so many people hadn't gotten into serious new relationships or been in any that had lasted. It was one of the reasons why Bastian barely spoke to his surviving family members, he was too scared about them dying and the sheer pain of that to get too close to them.

After the death of his brother, Bastian couldn't allow himself to go through that agony again.

But then if the Germans and stupid Hitler really were preparing for another war, then was it right for him to get into a relationship with Alice? They might have a great connection but it was surely doomed to die in the war.

Bastian shook his head. He couldn't put himself through that, or most importantly he couldn't put Alice through that if he died in the next few years.

Bastian couldn't handle the idea of this beautiful woman being in so much pain, agony and torment over his death.

Then Alice simply grabbed his hand and gently rubbed it. "We're both survived a lot worse in the war, haven't we?"

Bastian simply looked at the beautiful woman in front of him. This beautiful woman that had been captured, attacked and killed Germans with her bare hands. This beautiful woman that had seen so much but survived it all. And most importantly, she was a beautiful woman who didn't shy away from danger.

Bastian knew full well that Alice could have done what the French, British and Italian Governments would do. She could have simply looked away and pretended that nothing was going to happen, but she didn't.

Instead this amazing woman probably didn't even need to find courage because courage was who she was. She didn't cower in the face of the invasion of Rhineland, she took action and she did something.

Bastian nodded. "I will join your network even if you aren't my handler. And even if you don't want to explore whatever I feel between us, I will *always* have your back,"

Alice smiled and looked around. "I think Mary-Madeline and the others will be glad to hear that. There's lot of work to do and not a lot of time to do it in,"

As Alice leant closer and started talking about what they needed to do, what he needed to do whenever he went into Germany and the future of their spy network, Bastian just smiled.

Not because the future was going to be easy, always fun or certain. But because he just knew that him and Alice were going to be working together and exploring each other (in more ways than one) for a long, long time.

***

Paris, France
7th May 1945

Alice leant against the wonderfully warm railings of her little black balcony of her apartment as she looked out on her beautifully liberated Paris. She wore a brand new dark blue dressing gown, and Bastian wrapped his sensationally strong muscular arms around her.

Even after the chaos and troubles and adventures they had had together over the past nine years, Alice still wouldn't have had it any other way. They had both infiltrated Nazi headquarters, freed prisoners of war and in the past year they had helped get the all important map of France's northern coastline containing all the details of the defences into British hands, so the Allied forces knew exactly what to expect on D-Day.

As the sounds of people cheering, singing and screaming in utter delight echoed all over Paris, France and most probably the rest of the world. Alice couldn't believe that the war finally over and she was finally able to live in peace.

Alice loved the feeling of Bastian's hard body against hers as even years of war hadn't dulled their love for each other. They had kissed, rolled around in plenty of beds together and even gotten married again, and that just made Alice damn well proud of herself.

It was only in that little café on the day her and Bastian first met that she realised how badly she had loved and missed her husband. She almost felt like she was betraying him, but she had been so young when she had lost him, and he definitely would have wanted her to find love again.

Alice loved how Bastian was so close to her on her balcony that she felt his warm minty-fresh breath on her neck. The street below was filled with hundreds, if not thousands, of happy French people waving French flags and ripping down any Nazi flags that dared to still stand. For this was no longer the occupied zone, Vichy or any nonsense from the war, this was France.

And France would always be free.

As Bastian gently spun her around and started kissing her, Alice simply melted into him. She kissed him back hard. There had been so much death, war and bloodshed over the past few years that Alice simply wanted to be amongst the living once more and block out any memories of the past.

For that was what the past was and hopefully would remain this time, the idea of global conflicts had to remain in the past, and Alice just hoped that her new secret job for the French Government would help her to do that. She wasn't too hopeful, but she was definitely hopeful about one thing.

She truly could do anything with the amazingly beautiful sexy Bastian by her side, and she just knew that they would last forever because their love had survived a war, endless spy missions and even a few captures along the way.

If that wasn't a test of love and dedication, then Alice seriously didn't want to find out what was.

LOVE IN THE TRINITITE
Classified Date, 2022

Kavir Desert, Iran

British Intelligence Officer Adeline Zouch sat in a very uncomfortable and boiling hot seat of the top-secret military plane she was flying in over the desert in Iran. She hated being the only person in the long metal tube that the pilots called a hull and the deafening roar of the engines didn't relax her.

Adeline even hated the horrible scents of burning oil, sweat and bitter coffee that filled the air in the hull. It was such a disgusting way to travel that Adeline really wanted this Queen-forsaken mission to just be over already.

Adeline had never liked Iran or the middle east very much. Sure she knew it was a very dangerous area but she had always loved playing against the Russians and Chinese, because they had great spies. And that was what being a spy was truly about, playing games against your enemies.

The Russian and Chinese were clever, evil and fascinating people that Adeline loved to hunt down and investigate. It was only last week she had been tracking down the former head of Chinese Intelligence who had gone rogue. And Adeline was sure the Chinese Government would deny this but it was just flat out funny to see the Chinese Ambassador beg the UK government to take him out.

That was probably the only time Adeline had ever seen the Chinese play by the international rules and not actually go rogue. It was impressive, scary and just funny all at the same time.

The deafening sound of the engines roar and thunder and pop deep into the desert made Adeline's stomach tighten into a painful knot. The only reason why she was on the mission in the first place was because she hadn't been given new missions yet and the Prime Minister (also known as Mr Dickhead) apparently wanted the best person on this mission.

Adeline didn't agree in the slightest.

The mission was apparently simple, according to the exact same people who had never ever done any fieldwork or even fired a gun before, Adeline needed to go into the Kavir Desert and search for traces of a substance known as Trinitite.

Adeline had heard of the substance that was created when soil was superheated following a nuclear explosion, but this was hardly worth her time. She had investigated tons of Russian and Chinese nuclear testing facilities over the past decade, so sadly she was familiar with the substance.

Yet there were other agents who could have done this, but Adeline knew that the quicker she got this done. The sooner she could return to dealing with the Russians and Chinese agents that seemed to get more and more powerful each day, not that the UK Government was actually interested in the slightest.

Adeline held on tight as the military-transport plane banked a little and she just knew that she would be at her destination sooner or later.

All she actually knew about her mission destination was that it was a very remote stretch of desert that even the insurgents and local terrorist groups rarely went into because it was so dry and lifeless. At best Adeline would see a few animals and maybe a government patrol if this was a nuclear testing facility. At worse, the whole bloody Iranian army would be there.

Adeline had made sure she looked the part of a tourist just in case she was caught. She liked wearing her stab-proof vest, sandy shorts and hiking boots. Then Adeline picked up her small rucksack that was filled with wonderfully cool water, a gun and small satellite phone to call for an extraction when she needed it.

But her stomach still filled with butterflies as she felt the plane descend ever so slightly.

Non-spies would probably call her paranoid or something but she just knew that something was off.

There was something about the extreme heat and the uncomfortableness of the air that made the entire mission feel not right.

The intelligence reports might believe that the deserts were always empty, but that was a lie. The fall of Afghanistan had proved how bad some intelligence reports could be, Adeline just really, really hoped that this wasn't one of those times.

Because if there were a lot of enemies in the desert then there would be no extraction, help or support this time. She would be well and truly alone and as much as the idea of fighting the enemies of the UK excited her, Adeline knew that these enemies wouldn't take her prisoner in the slightest.

They would kill her.

Slowly.

***

Classified Date, 2022
Kavir Desert, Iran

Former British Intelligence Officer Theo Martin really liked his brand new job working for private military contractors in the boiling, sweaty, cultural hub of Iran. He actually didn't mind this beautiful country in the slightest. Sure the country was run by crazies, extremists and corruption but the people weren't that bad. And the food was simply sensational.

Theo sat in the shadow created by a very, very tall sandstone column that seemed to rise out of the sandy desert ground just for him. Theo almost wished he was at one of the amazing little "cafes" that served him battery acid bitter coffee and sweet wonderful pastries that were specialities of Iran where he was staying. He simply loved it here.

The wonderful silence of the desert was another delightful gift away from the constant noise of the UK and MI6. And as a private military contractor he still got all his powers, gadgets and licence to kill without all the bureaucracy nonsense.

Theo loved staring out at the boiling hot desert with sand dunes that seemed to roll on for miles upon miles with sandstone columns rising up as a little scenic break to make the landscape more interesting.

The only bad thing about the desert was the awful boiling hot air that stunk of heat without a hint of moisture in it. It was simply awful to breathe and that was why he always had a humidifier on in his room, he just wanted to try and enjoy a little bit of moisture for a few minutes before the heat of the air simply made it pointless.

Theo didn't entirely know why his boss wanted him to come out here and look for Trinitite that silly little compound that was a result of nuclear explosions. Theo and everyone in the intelligence community knew exactly why the Iranians were building up their nuclear testing programme again. It was all because there was no Iran Nuclear Deal anymore so there was no incentive for them to not make nuclear weapons.

So they got excited about it and they were

building a lot. Theo had once read an intelligence report proposing Iran had bought enough nuclear material from Russia to build a hundred nuclear warheads.

Theo was sure in the slightest what proving it would actually achieve. What would the international community do with the proof? Simply slap Iran on the wrist and tell it was a bad country?

Granted Theo had read a report before he left his room today about the United Nations calling a meeting to attempt to create a new nuclear disarmament bill. And even the US, Russia and China were meant to sign it meaning they would have to get rid of about a quarter of their nuclear stock piles, so maybe that new Bill had been a possible cause for the need for this proof.

Theo didn't know. He just followed orders.

Theo just laughed because of how true it was. And that was one of the reasons why he had left MI6 because the entire lack of international justice and all that stuff just seemed so pointless after a while. But at least now he got a little more freedom.

A low humming sound got louder and louder from behind Theo and his stomach tensed. There weren't meant to be any patrols this early in the morning. There weren't meant to be any patrols at all today according to his contacts in the Iranian Government.

This was bad.

Theo slowly got up and peeked around the

sandstone column he was sitting behind and frowned when he saw a very large black military transport plane hover for a split second before taking off again.

Theo saw a very short woman was standing where the plane had been and she looked like a tourist perfectly. Theo was hardly impressed to have another spy in the mix, that would only complicate matters and considering she was playing the part of the tourist a little too well by wearing shorts (she would burn easily) she was definitely going to be a liability.

Granted the woman did look amazing as she started to walk over to the sandstone column, and she thankfully hadn't seen Theo yet. Theo seriously loved her fit sexy legs, amazingly toned body and her sexy smile that seemed to be lighting up the desert.

She looked amazing and her eyes were like sapphires in the desert sun, and Theo definitely liked her sensational blond hair (that was definitely dyed to match the hair of local women) that flapped about the wind so elegantly.

She was sheer perfection.

Theo almost felt embarrassed to be wearing a tanned loose-fitting shirt, trousers and hiking boots that probably highlighted how fit and muscular he was, but did nothing to make him look so attractive compared to this goddess walking in the desert.

They locked eyes.

As much as Theo wanted to stare into those stunning sapphire eyes. Theo's training kicked in.

He grabbed his gun from his back and aimed at her.

She did the same.

***

Classified Date, 2022
Kavir Desert, Iran

Adeline absolutely hated this awful desert and she was in no mood not to shoot this man.

He might have been extremely hot sexy and looked like the cover model of a GQ magazine. But this was her mission and even though he had the most kissable lips she had ever seen he was not going to stop her.

The insanely hot man slowly started to walk towards her and Adeline firmly held her finger on the trigger. She was definitely going to kill him if he tried to stop her.

Clearly the typical intelligence reports had been completely wrong and now it might cost Adeline her life. She was flat out not impressed.

"I got a little lost," Adeline said in perfect Arabic. "Do you know the way back to town?"

The insanely hot man laughed and spoke in English. "You don't speak a lot of Arabic, do you? Your accent is still too strong to form some of the sounds correctly,"

Adeline hated this man even more now. She was a highly trained operative of the UK Government, she had split the throats of greater men with just her bare fingernails. How dare he question her.

Adeline spoke in Chinese. "Sorry but who made you expert in everything Englishman?"

The hot man seemed to smile. Adeline had read a lot of faces in her time and she was surprised that the man was really smiling at her. He either liked her for some reason or he was an extremely good spy.

She had to be very careful around him.

"MI6?" the hot man asked.

"You first?" Adeline asked, pointing her gun firmly at his head.

"Private Military Contractor working for the UK Government. Authority Code: Alpha Lemur-666," he said.

That was not exactly what she wanted to hear. She didn't mind private contractors and she had worked with them before, just not in this ridiculous stupid heat. Sweat was already pouring off her forehead and rolling down her back.

All she wanted to do was get on with her mission and leave this Queen-forsaken place.

"Trinitite?" the man asked. "You know where it is,"

Adeline forced herself not to react. The mission was too important not to focus on, and this insanely hot sexy man could have easily tortured another private contractor to get the code. He could be an Iranian spy.

She couldn't trust him.

The man lowered his gun and put it into his back.

Adeline didn't do the same. "How do I know I can trust you?"

The man laughed. "We don't trust people in this spy game. But I wouldn't kill a fellow Brit for love or money,"

Adeline liked the idea of working with him for a little while and even the idea of that made her stomach fill with damn butterflies, and her hands turned sweaty unlike before.

Damn it. She could not fall for this insanely stunning man under any circumstances. Love and emotions on the field get people killed. It was as simple as that.

"Theo," the man said walking over to Adeline.

Adeline gestured with her gun to stay a few metres away from her. Then she put her gun away.

"Code name is Sarah," Adeline said.

Theo smiled. Adeline had to admit *Theo* was a hot name and now he was so close, she was amazed at how sexy and toned his body was under his slightly opened loose shirt.

Adeline started to walk off into the desert and headed towards a very tall sand dune that would give her the best possible vantage point over the area. She needed to see where would be the best location to detonate a nuclear bomb and create trinitite.

***

Classified Date, 2022
Kavir Desert, Iran

Theo was really impressed with the composure

and strength and beauty of this woman. Of course this beautiful angel was not called Sarah, he doubted she actually knew a woman called Sarah in the slightest. But she was a strong spy who had good instincts.

Theo and Sarah stood on top of a very large sand dune that somehow beautiful Sarah had just managed to storm up like it was nothing. Theo had slipped over twice because the damn sand had moved so much.

Sarah was carefully scanning the horizon and local area like she was some kind of building expert who knew exactly what each and every dip and ridge in the desert landscape meant. Theo didn't have that much of a clue about geography but clearly that was why he needed this woman called Sarah.

The air was still boiling hot but now Theo was sweating for a different reason entirely. He was sweating because being this close to this stunning beauty was just too much to bear.

"You born in Southern England?" Theo asked. "Can hear it in your voice,"

Sarah weakly smiled. "You don't sound like a former Officer at times,"

Theo was falling for this amazing woman more and more with each passing second. Clearly this woman was trained very well, most people rarely recognised that he was former MI6 these days, but this woman clearly knew him a lot more than he would like to admit.

Not necessarily a bad thing though.

"Want to know why I left?" Theo asked.

Sarah laughed. "I already know why. Everyone leaves for the same reason. You left because you wanted the freedom to do what you wanted in the name of Queen and country and most importantly you wanted proper equipment and pay unlike the cheap government things MI6 gives you,"

Theo just stared at Sarah's amazingly kissable lips. She didn't sound like she bought or accepted the reason at all, but at least she had been willing to listen to other people say it. Most of Theo's former friends had banished him, kicked him to the curb and just wished him dead when he had told them he was leaving for a private company.

This sexy woman seemed to be different.

"This way," Sarah said pointing to the bottom of the sand dune they were standing on.

Theo and Sarah started to walk down the dune together and Theo asked about why they were heading in this way. Even if the woman wasn't into him, he at least needed to learn from her for future missions,

"When an atomic bomb goes off or is tested, imagine the extreme force that is created. It creates trinitite which we're looking for. But it would also create a shockwave that would destroy old dunes and create new much taller sand dunes,"

Theo looked at what they were walking on for a moment. Now he actually gave the idea the time of day, it seriously made perfect sense why the sand dune they were walking on was strange and out of place. It was much larger than most of the other sand dunes.

In fact this had to be at least another five metres tall that the other sand dunes in the area. And considering the winds and extreme heat of the local desert that was a very strange fact indeed.

But at least one of the benefits of walking down an extremely tall sand dune was that it created a lot of shade one side, and thankfully Theo and Sarah were walking down that same side.

Theo loved the delightfully cool shade for a few more moments until they reached the bottom of the dune.

"Now we start looking?" Theo asked.

Sarah simply smiled almost like this was some kind of amazing treasure hunt. Theo wasn't exactly sure how amazing it was going to be.

But he was definitely excited about the treasure hunt.

And he was a lot more excited about spending time with Sarah than he wanted to admit.

A lot more.

***

Classified Date, 2022

Kavir Desert, Iran

After a few hours of searching, resting in the shade and drinking plenty of water, Adeline and Theo were just about to give up this utterly ridiculous mission by walking over to another very large sand dune that was almost a hundred metres away from the dune they had walked down earlier, when Adeline felt something under her feet.

Given how they had both been walking, getting to know each other and resting for the past few hours, Adeline absolutely hated to admit it but she knew what the horrible desert felt like under her feet. The desert always felt hot, made her feet sweat and it felt like a constantly moving ocean of sand particles.

But this felt a lot more solid.

Adeline stopped dead in her tracks and she actually didn't care about the boiling hot sun beaming down on her as she looked at insanely hot Theo.

He didn't seem to understand what she was getting at as she smiled at him. But his lack of understanding didn't make him look bad in her eyes, over the past few hours this hot sexy man had told her about past missions, his family and life. Things that no spy was ever meant to talk about, and he included such little details that no background story ever included.

He had been telling her the truth.

As Theo knelt down and started to dig around in the sand, definitely smiling at the coolness of the sand under the surface, Adeline just focused on him.

She had come on this mission because she had been told to and she had hated it from the start. She hadn't wanted to be in this Queen-forsaken country, hunting down Trinitite and the rest. But she had instead found a beautiful man that she felt amazingly comfortable with.

"Down here," Theo said.

Adeline knelt down and hissed as the sheer intense heat of the sand shot into her knees and she started digging.

It didn't take too long for them to dig ten centimetres under the boiling surface to find a massive cool chunk of glassy-rocky Trinitite.

The discovery slammed into Adeline like a ton of bricks. This confirmed every single person's worse fears about the Iranians and that they were not only building nuclear weapons but testing them.

And for the soil to get superheated enough to form Trinitite then that meant that these weapon tests were very, very successful.

Adeline watched Theo as he broke a large chunk of Trinitite off and handed it to her. She hesitated for a moment and then she just stared into his amazingly soft eyes.

The rest of the chunk of Trinitite was far too thick and chunky to break off another piece without the right equipment. You would certainly need a sledgehammer to break it up anymore.

Adeline was amazed that Theo had just given her the key to both their missions. Theo was allowing her to go home a hero, but he would go home a disappointment.

It wasn't logical in the slightest but a simple chunk of Trinitite highlighted the trouble with spies and relationships. There was no winning for a couple.

Even if Adeline and Theo did start a relationship, they worked for different people and it was no secret that MI6 and private companies hated each other. The relationship would never work out and neither one of them was going to leave their jobs.

Adeline took out her gun from her rucksack. Pointing it at the chunk of Trinitite.

"What are you doing?" Theo asked.

Adeline smiled at him. "The bullet should be strong enough to break the Trinitite in half so we can both return as heroes. There are no enemies in the area and even if there were my extraction would be here before they arrived,"

Theo frowned. "Exactly. *Your* extraction,"

Adeline gasped as she realised what she had done. It was just training and her training had always taught her that herself and her mission was always the most important. Even when she had worked with MI5, CIA and FBI in the past, *her* mission was always more important than the joint mission.

She just didn't want it to be this way with Theo, the sexy man she had actually dared to open her heart to.

"Come back with me," Adeline said. "My boss will go mad. Your boss will go mad. But I'll be happy,"

Adeline hadn't meant to say it but it just felt so natural and true. And truth was a rarity in the spy game. Adeline needed Theo to make her happy, at least that's what she wanted.

The distant sound of motorbikes and 4x4 jeeps echoed against the silence of the desert.

"What do you say?" Adeline asked as she smiled.

She would love to get into a firefight with the Iranians but this wasn't the time. Not with the Trinitite mission coming first and she couldn't risk putting her Theo in danger.

Theo whipped out his gun and pressed it against the Trinitite. He fired. Breaking the Trinitite in two.

Adeline wanted to smile but she grabbed the Satellite phone from her rucksack and entered the phone number to summon her extraction.

Adeline picked up her piece of Trinitite and Theo did the same then they ran out away from the dune so the extraction plane could easily see them.

The sound of 4x4 jeeps and motorbikes got louder and louder. Clearly the Iranians were back to check on their experiments.

Adeline saw little black dots move in the distance and come over dunes and ridges and she knew that time was running out.

A massive roar screamed overhead as a massive black military transport plane descended.

Adeline and Theo prepared themselves to jump onto the descending cargo ramp as the plane itself descended.

Gunshots echoed around the desert.

Adeline climbed onto the cargo ramp and pulled herself up.

The pilot started to take off.

Adeline panicked.

She reached down to get Theo. Theo grabbed her hand.

Bullets smashed into him. Theo screamed.

Adeline pulled him up. Theo's blood dripped out.

"Get us the fuck out of here!" Adeline shouted.

***

Classified Date, 2022

Top-Secret Location, England

The sweet fruity smells of apples, pineapples and limes filled the air from delightful cleaning chemicals as Theo awoke in a bright blue hospital bed barely covered up by its pathetically thin sheets.

Theo hadn't been in a hospital room for ages but he definitely knew this was an expensive one with its smart TV hanging on the wall, bowl of fruit on the bedside table next to him and a very nice vase of roses that looked brand new.

There was a window on the other side of the room but Theo didn't care to look. He was just glad to be alive for a change, but he was definitely going to miss whatever pain medication the doctors had him on. He had once been shot in the chest and stomach and a local Afghan doctor who was helping the West had stitched him up and hid him for four days.

Those were the worse four days of his life, but those Afghans were amazing people.

"You're awake then," a familiar woman said.

It took Theo a few moments to notice that beautiful Adeline with her stunning sapphire eyes was standing and looking out of the window.

"Good view?" Theo asked.

Adeline didn't even turn around. "I would like the view behind me, but I'm currently watching some Royal Air Force Pilots argue about something. It's rather interesting,"

Theo just smiled. He didn't know why in the slightest but she was just such an amazing woman. He loved how she was so strong, capable and she had saved his life.

He had no idea what the MI6's and his company's reports would say later, but he knew the truth. The truth was *Sarah* (he had to find out her real name) could have simply dropped him and let him fall to the desert below when he had been shot.

That was actually protocol and what you were meant to do.

But this amazingly intelligent, stunning woman had taken a risk for him by helping him onto the plane. That took some guts considering how snobbish her bosses were probably about letting an "outsider" into their ranks.

"You were out for three days," Sarah said. "I admit I wasn't always here during the day. I had to meet your boss, my boss and talk to our UN Ambassador,"

"Did we find the Trinitite?" Theo asked.

Sarah came over and leant over Theo's bed. He

felt his hands turn sweaty and sticky and his stomach filled with butterflies.

"Yep. The lab reports confirmed and now the West is leading sanctions against Iran, and even Russia and China are sanctioning Iran without any conditions,"

Theo smiled that was beyond strange, but the reason was clear enough to anyone who studied geopolitics. At the end of the day, Russia and China only wanted themselves to be the nuclear superpowers so whilst they struggled to get the UK, USA and the rest of Europe under control, those two states would have to be happy with stopping Iran from becoming a true nuclear power.

Theo took Sarah's hand and rubbed it gently. He was surprised at how smooth it was and he really loved the amazing chemistry that flowed between them.

"What did our bosses say?" Theo asked.

"Well your boss is a sexist dick so I broke his nose when he copped a feel," Sarah said.

Theo was hardly impressed but he was equally hardly surprised. There was a reason why there were so few female intelligence officers in his company.

"And my boss wasn't exactly pleased we worked together but he admitted it was clear we got results. And he was impressed I handled your boss and our UN ambassador so well,"

Theo tried to lean closer to her but pain from his bullet wounds pulsed up and down him in a momentary wave of agony.

"What's their proposal?" Theo asked.

He loved the sound of Sarah's laugh and they both knew how spies agencies worked a little too well.

"If you're willing they want us to work together," Sarah said with an amazing smile.

Theo just nodded without any hesitation. He would love getting a chance to know, work and maybe even love with this amazing woman.

"Brilliant," Sarah said with a lot more enthusiasm than Theo reckoned she was used to.

Theo was surprised by Sarah's hug and then her nose touched his and she just smiled.

"Adeline," she said.

Theo shrugged. Was that the name of their new target? Code name? Mission?

"My name is Adeline," she said.

Theo felt his heart skip a few beats as he realised how impossibly hard that must have been for her, and he was so grateful she trusted him enough to share it.

Working with her was going to be amazing fun.

***

Classified Date, 2022
Top-Secret Location, England

A few months year after travelling to China, Russia and the Middle East again, Adeline was so amazed and in love with her insanely hot sexy man. Adeline was amazed at how smart he was, able to pick up and blend with different cultures and languages so seamlessly that regardless of his skin colour he could be a local anywhere in the world.

They made a perfect team. Adeline loved not only Theo's smarts but also how he carried himself with such ease and confidence that he never looked out of place. It was the perfect partner for her own deadliness and passion and playing cat-and-mouse with foreign agents.

It was certainly a different pace from chasing down terrorists in the middle east but Adeline was more than glad sexy Theo was adapting quickly.

So as Adeline sat on a very uncomfortable plastic chair in a large metal hangar in a top-secret airport waiting for their plane to arrive to travel off to another mission, Adeline just felt so alive.

Her beautiful Theo was talking with their handler about the next mission and he really did look so special. After being alone for a decade and hunting down the Queen's enemies by herself, Adeline never believed she could work with someone.

But as Theo smiled at her, a true loving smile, Adeline was so glad she had found him because spy work was a lot more fun, exciting and interesting with a partner.

And no matter what the future threw at them, Adeline knew she would be fine and safe and loved, because she had Theo by her side. And he had her by his.

And Adeline was still surprised that it was all only possible because of some silly Trinitite and a boiling hot desert.

Definitely about as spy-like a meet-cute could get, and Adeline loved it.

LOVING THE CORPORATE
20th July 2022

Southern England, United Kingdom

Professional Corporate Spy Anna Smith sat on a very uncomfortable bus seat surrounded by her follow beauty product factory workers in all their outfits, height and sizes as they all talked and laughed with each other about their busy workday ahead.

Anna simply looked out the window and watched the rich beautiful English countryside roll past them as the little bus drove onwards to the factory in the middle of nowhere. She wasn't exactly keen on her fellow workers after the past six months, but a job was certainly that. Just a job.

Normally in July Anna tended to focus more on spying on ice cream, holiday agencies and sun cream makers because it was about summer time when the rivals pay extremely good money for information. But even Anna loved a good sob story from time to time.

So when a client contacted her through her

extremely encrypted email address and told her the story about a local factory that was brainwashing their workers into mindless drones and poisoning the soil, leading to crop failure for the local villages. Anna was a little more interested in this potential job.

Granted she was hardly impressed by the sheer stink of some of the workers with their constant and immensely strong body odour, smell of alcohol and cheap whiskey on their breath. But they all seemed to be good people, and the management seemed to be even better.

She couldn't completely understand why her employer, who had already paid her a hundred thousand pounds, believed the workers were being brainwashed. Yet her employer was right about one thing, the upper-upper management was mysterious and mystical and definitely hiding something.

The bus shook a little as it turned onto a dirt road and Anna rolled her eyes as she knew that they would soon all be at the factory.

It had taken Anna six months just to get into the main production area of the factory instead of being in the office section. Yet even the office was rather fascinating because all the documents, invoices and other essential paperwork seemed perfect to the untrained eye. But Anna knew a lot better.

Someone in upper-upper management was forging the paperwork that was later sent to investors (who invested up to a million pounds a year) and government agencies.

This was fraud on a massive scale.

Anna just smiled to herself as she got more and more excited about her day ahead. After she had managed to… prevent the normal worker from taking the upper management their afternoon tea, Anna had spiked the tea, cakes and scones with eyedrops so needlessly to say the management would be very ill today.

That was why Anna always made a point to carry round a green fanny pack that looked like a first aid kit. It always contained official first aid supplies and underneath were a bunch of spy equipment. Like knock-out drops, a USB drive with password unlocking software and a little EMP device that her ex-husband made her one Christmas in case she ever needed to knock out a building's power supplies.

He really was amazing back in the day.

Anna was more than excited about finally getting a chance to go into the management's office, look around and finally get some proof on what was going on. And ideally she would be able to find out who was behind this fraud and corporation.

Her fellow factory workers started to get more and more excited as the bus started to drive up a gravel road, and the workers could see the very top of the factory that was situated in the valley below.

As much as Anna smiled every morning to look like the rest of her fellow workers, every morning she felt her stomach twist in both excitement and fear. She had been doing spying too long to get easily caught so that was hardly a problem. Her real concern was getting caught and never being able to deliver the justice that her employers hired her for.

That was her only fear.

And if she got caught then it meant she would never be able to see her beautiful little daughter again who she visited once a month when her ex-husband allowed her to. It wasn't that they didn't get on, it was just he wasn't exactly a fan of her work.

She couldn't exactly disagree with his reasons, that was why Anna just wanted to live in a world where these corporations weren't so corrupt and dangerous and polluting. And all that one day might affect her precious little girl.

Anna wished more than anything else in the world that she could have enough money one day to buy a little ranch for her and her daughter. Her daughter was obsessed with horses and it was definitely beyond a phase, Anna just wanted to be a good mother.

The bus slowed to a stop and Anna smiled. It was time to get to work and Anna was really looking forward to stopping this factory once and for all and definitely helping to make the world a better place for her daughter.

She just hoped no idiot was going to get in her way.

***

20th July 2022
Southern England, United Kingdom

Amateur Corporate Spy Joshua McDonald was waiting at the god-awful gates of the immense beauty product factory that looked like a large cuboid building as he waited for the bus of workers to arrive.

He leant against the hot metal of the factory and liked the almost burning sensations of the metal heating up his skin through his blue worker's uniform. He hated the entire factory, people and management.

But he was here for a purpose.

The stupid factory had popped up nine months ago and immediately cleared all government checks within days (a process that was meant to take a year) and then within a week the factory started pumping out toxic chemicals into the local river that went straight into the farms.

The local farms and surrounding areas used to smell amazing and Joshua loved hiking the footpaths as a teenager with the refreshing hints of apples, pine and ferns that filled the air. Yet now the entire area just smelt of horrible chemicals, rotting fish and rotting plants from where the water was killing the local environment.

The local villages and wildlife couldn't last much longer.

Joshua hated everything about this situation. He hated how he had seen so many of his friends in the local village lose their farms, crops and livelihoods all because of a corrupt factory. Then the teenagers started to get sick, then the women and now the men.

Everyone in the village was slowly starting to get sicker and sicker and all the governmental officials denied it was to do with the factory.

Joshua wanted nothing more than to burn the entire place to the ground. He wanted to kill the entire management, but as his mother had said before she died two months after the factory opened *violence was never the way*. It was such a motherly thing to say, but she was right.

Damn her.

Joshua had slowly worked his way into the factory, becoming a good worker and gaining the trust of the management. There was a rumour going round that Joshua was meant to be promoted any moment now and that would give him access to exactly what he needed.

He had an ex-girlfriend at a national newspaper that had promised to leak the story to the public if he got her some proof.

Even as he waited for the bus to turn up Joshua felt so nervous. His knees were shaking, his heart was pounding and his breathing was rapid.

He needed today to go perfectly so he could get the promotion and get access to the files he needed so he could prove to the world (or local authorities at least) that this factory was a monstrous place.

The sound of something hitting the gravel road in the distance made Joshua weakly smile, because soon the workers would be here.

He knew it was a silly fear but every single day he

feared that someone new was going to get on that bus who was a spy hunter or something, and that same person could catch him and damn him and his family and local villages to death.

Joshua's phone buzzed and he took it out and rolled his eyes when he saw it was a text message from his manager.

He read the message and smiled when it told him the security codes to the main office because they were mysteriously ill today, so he was temporarily manager. He was a one man band running everything that five people normally ran.

Joshua didn't really care too much because after today he would have his proof and then he would be in the wind.

Then his phone buzzed again and Joshua cursed under his breath. He was still in charge but the head of the factory and corporation was heading there to keep a close eye on everything.

Joshua had never met the big boss but from subtle whispers and murmurs from other workers, the big boss was not a good man, not kind and definitely not the type of person you wanted to screw over.

Joshua was tempted to cancel his plans for today but this was the best shot he had had in the past five months of working here. He didn't know if he was going to get this chance again. He needed to try.

The large bus filled with workers drove into the factory compound and Joshua smiled at all of them as they popped off the bus and looked so excited about starting the day.

Joshua was about to call them all over to him when someone caught his eye.

A tall elegant woman popped off the bus and Joshua's mouth just stopped working. She was the most beautiful woman he had ever seen and there was just something about her.

Joshua flat out loved her long slender legs, long brown hair that perfectly framed her circular head and strong jawline. She easily could have been a model in another life and she certainly could have had any man she wanted.

And Joshua seriously loved how she carried herself with such pride, confidence and like she was in complete control. She was like some sort of god walking amongst little human ants that she could easily deal with if she wanted. Not in an arrogant way, but in a way that made Joshua drawn to her.

He had seen the woman about a few times but there was something different about her today. She wasn't normally this confident or maybe she was and she was just hiding it better.

Whoever this woman was, she definitely didn't belong here. All the other workers seemed really happy and drawn to be here, but none of them were confident or felt in control. No one in the local area did as they were all waiting for their own damnation because of this factory.

This woman was different.

And as hot and sexy as she was. She terrified

Joshua.

He couldn't let her get in his way. And that was a promise.

***

20th July 2022
Southern England, United Kingdom

A few hours later, Anna was extremely impressed by her amazing, if not a little out-there, plan with the eyedrops had actually worked so perfectly. All five managers were out sick with extreme bowel problems and that was just flat out perfect.

As it was approaching lunchtime and everyone who the time the normal managers went to lunch (so she couldn't see why this new temporary manager who she hadn't met yet would be any different), Anna had slipped away from the production line and had made it into a long grey corridor on the top floor of the factory.

Anna wasn't a fan of the god awful grey paint job that covered the smooth walls of the corridor and even the bright blue fire-doors that were the entrances into the main offices weren't attractive. Anna could still hear the factory below her and she was hardly impressed that the noise of the factory machines were so loud it would be difficult to hear if someone was returning or walking about up here.

From her position on the production line from earlier, Anna had managed to get a clear view of the staircase up to the top floor, and by her count everyone was meant to be up here wasn't at the moment.

That was another advantage of paying off the chef yesterday to cook something very special for the workers, managers and even the big boss if he decided to show up. Anna wasn't exactly sure how the hell you were meant to pronounce it, but what she understood was that the chef knew the management liked some special French dish.

So he was cooking it, and it had drawn a crowd.

Anna carefully went along the long corridor and subtly checked to see if any of the doors were open, and surprisingly enough most of them were. She wouldn't have minded going into some of them just in case they were useful.

But the only office of interest up here was the main office used by the management themselves. The rest of the offices were all Human Resources, Accounts Payable and Bookkeeping. Not exactly what Anna wanted at the moment.

The sound of someone walking up the stairs made Anna roll her eyes and she quickly dipped into one of the other offices with the open doors. Keeping it just open enough to hide her but make sure she could still see the person.

Anna wasn't impressed with the smell of cheesy feet that filled the little box office that was used by an accountant judging by the finance books on the desk.

A few moments later a very fit man walked past wearing a blue worker's uniform. Anna had sort of seen him before but never really looked at him. He was so beautiful and handsome with his tight ass, tight uniform that highlighted how skinny he was with some muscles around his biceps and calves, and there was just something rather stunning about him.

Anna supposed he was the new temporary manager and with those looks she definitely would have minded following him. Yet it was strange how he was up here in the middle of lunchtime, as a manager (even if only temporary) it was expected of him not to be up here.

He could have forgotten something important that he needed, but that wasn't how any manager worked in all the corporations Anna had spied on.

He was up to something.

The hot man went up to the very end of the corridor, took out a key and opened the door to the main office.

Anna wouldn't have had a problem opening the door because of the tools in her fanny pack, but this stunning man was troubling her now. Why was he going into the main office during lunchtime?

Heavy footsteps pounded up the staircase and Anna felt her stomach twist. Something was wrong here.

Anna went into her fanny pack and got out a little device that looked like a smartphone. It was technically a smartphone but she had added a lot of software to it recently. Including an app that scanned for radio signals.

Anna was seriously not impressed when radio

signals were being sent from the main office to someone from inside the factory. Chances are that the handsome man triggered some kind of alarm when he entered the office.

That's why Anna always scanned important offices before she went inside because now someone knew that handsome man was up to something. That meant security would get tighter and her mission would be even harder.

Not good.

A few moments later an extremely overweight man stomped down the corridor and Anna wanted to be sick as she smelt his immense body odour. The man was wearing a large, unflattering suit that only highlighted how overweight he was.

"Ouch!" the handsome man shouted.

Anna carefully watched as the overweight man grabbed the handsome man by the collar of his uniform, grabbed the key from him and spat at his face.

"I'm calling the police you little shit!" he shouted. "You try stealing from and I'll gut you if the cops don't get here soon enough. I gutted peeps before. You'll be no different,"

Anna almost wanted to laugh at all the trouble the handsome amateur was getting himself into but then the overweight man dragged the handsome amateur over to the office she was hiding in.

Anna ducked behind the door as it opened and the overweight man through the hot amateur inside.

He locked the door behind him.

Anna simply smiled at the hot amateur as he looked dumbfounded at her. This was going to be amazing fun.

***

20th July 2022
Southern England, United Kingdom

Joshua was absolutely steaming about getting caught by the big boss idiot himself. He didn't know how he had been so stupid but now everything was completely at risk.

And to make matters even worse, he was completely trapped in a little account office with an extremely hot beautiful woman who just smiled at him.

Joshua recognised her as the beautiful woman from the bus and even now she looked so relaxed, confident and like she was in complete control. Joshua didn't know who she was exactly but she was amazing. And even with the office heating up more and more and Joshua's palms were sweaty, she still looked as cool as a cucumber.

"Anna Smith, Corporate spy at ya service," she said extending out her hand.

Joshua was so confused. She was clearly just stupid or something because if she was really a spy then why the hell did she just admit it so easily? Surely that was against the spy code or something.

The hot woman gestured him to shake her hand. He did.

"A little weak of a handshake but acceptable," the woman said, her smile only growing.

It was only then that Joshua realised she didn't let go of his hand. Her hand was so silky smooth and beautiful and Joshua even felt like sexual energy was flowing between them. He really, really liked her. Joshua even wanted to hold a little more of her.

Then he forced himself to let go, the woman looked slightly disappointed.

"Corporate spy?" Joshua asked. "Why are you here?"

"Judging by your accent you're very local. I surveyed the local area before I started my mission. I presume you want the same evidence as me but our reasons are different," Anna said leaning against the wall by the door.

Joshua felt his stomach fill with butterflies. Anna was clearly as smart as they come but they needed to get out of here and get the proof.

Joshua went for the door and Anna gently placed her hand on his and shook her head.

He didn't want to back away from the door but for some reason he just trusted this woman.

"I'm Joshua," he said.

Beautiful Anna smiled and nodded her thanks for sharing that with her. Then Anna took a few steps back.

"I'm getting paid a lot of money to do this job," Anna said. "I don't need an amateur screwing it up,"

Joshua frowned. "This isn't about a job or

money! This is about my friends, family and community that is dying!"

Anna nodded slowly like she was mulling something over in her mind. Joshua hated it when people did that normally but on her it looked so cute.

"I understand that. I saw it for myself. I just… have my own reasons for why this job cannot fail," Anna said looking at the floor.

Joshua had seen that look too many times on his mother's face before she died. It was the sort of look you give someone when the truth was too painful to reveal.

Joshua gently went over to her and lifted up her chin so the two of them looked into each other's eyes. And Anna certainly had some great lifeful eyes that Joshua didn't mind looking into.

"What's wrong? And how can I help?" Joshua asked.

Anna looked almost shocked and confused by his offer, Joshua didn't know her very well but he could tell she was in pain, and very beautiful. She was the last person he ever wanted to be in pain.

Anna gently pushed him away and started studying the door frame.

"My daughter. She's ten right now and loves horses," Anna said. "My ex-husband loves me and her but he doesn't agree with my work so our relationship could never work out. I just want to get enough money to give her the life she deserves,"

Joshua could only nod. He definitely knew the

feeling from a child's viewpoint. His own parents had fought a lot, argued and barely agreed on anything so his father was hardly about. And it definitely made childhood a little less fun, interesting and solid.

Joshua had always felt like he had been missing half of himself until he became an adult.

He was definitely going to help her. Not only because she was beautiful but because it was the right thing to do.

Joshua placed a loving hand on her shoulder. "What can I do to help?"

Anna gave him a seductive smile. "Let me to do my job and don't fuck it up again,"

Joshua wanted to be offended but there was just something so seductive and fun about her words. He could only smile.

Anna took out something from her bright green fanny pack that looked like a key and she pressed it into the door. The key-like device hummed a little then the door unlocked itself.

Joshua didn't know where in the hell she got it from or whether it was legal or not. But he was very excited to see what other incredible things she could do.

Anna went into the corridor and he followed without hesitation.

***

20th July 2022

Southern England, United Kingdom

Knowing the utterly silly mistake that beautiful

Joshua had made, Anna was never ever going to make the same mistake as him. She was professional and now she had a stunning sidekick, the pressure was even more on to complete the mission.

The moment Anna reached the large blue firedoor at the end of the grey corridor she took out her smartphone again and scanned for radio signals. Just as she suspected the big boss had increased security.

There were currently scanners monitoring every inch of the main office, storage areas and every other millimetre of the factory where people were not meant to be.

Just in case the corridor they were standing in would soon be scanned, Anna activated a special feature of her smartphone that sent out radio signals that caused the scanners to report that everything was okay no matter what.

Anna smiled when her phone reported it was working. Her spy gadgets were amazing and she seriously loved her job.

A very quiet gasp behind her made her smile even more as beautiful Joshua was also clearly impressed.

Anna took out her little key device that moulded itself to any lock and the main office door opened with a simple click.

They went inside.

The main office was a lot larger and emptier than she had first imagined. She had pictured the office containing endless rows of computers, files and other office-y things. But this office only had a single desk and computer.

Anna stopped Joshua when he was about to rush over to the computer and she carefully scanned the ground with her eyes and smartphone to make sure there were no more surprises.

Thankfully there were none so Anna and Joshua went over to the large computer and Joshua cursed that it was locked.

She was really starting to lose hope with him because he was such an amateur. He was hot as hell but not a very good corporate spy.

Yet she supposed she might as well ask just in case he knew something she didn't.

"What's wrong?" Anna asked.

"The security codes I got texted earlier mentioned how you can only put it each code once before a full system wipe starts. It's a protocol to stop people like us,"

Anna wasn't exactly impressed with the term *us* but that didn't matter right now. This was just another problem they faced because even her password decoder would technically enter the password more than once and that could trigger the wiping programme.

Joshua thankfully got out his phone and huffed.

"The password for the main computer isn't included," Joshua said. "The management only gave me the passwords to the computers in the bookkeeping, accountants and human resources,"

Anna rolled her eyes. This wasn't what they needed. Any moment that big boss idiot was going to return and find them, and Anna didn't like violence in the slightest.

"Text your boss and get the password. Make up some excuse or something," Anna said.

Joshua nodded and texted his boss. Something about needing to access records because a government official turned up for a surprise inspection.

"For God sake," Joshua said.

Anna smiled. The boss had texted him saying that get the big boss idiot to sort it out.

"Use your decoder," Joshua said looking defeated.

Anna wanted to but she could see how much it was paining Joshua. He wanted to succeed but he also needed to make sure that the evidence was intact. This was a massive risk for both of them.

But Anna did what he said.

The computer unlocked straight away.

Joshua gently moved her away and thankfully he knew exactly where the secret files were located.

"Wow," Joshua said.

Anna agreed as Joshua pulled up the real environment reports, confidential emails and even health reports about the certainty of destroying the local environment.

This was exactly the proof they needed.

Anna took out the last USB she had in her fanny

pack that contained an automatic transmitter that used satellites to send the information to her personal computers back at home. That if she didn't send a special password within six hours would send the information to every single news outlet in the country.

Joshua started transferring some of the documents to an email address and Anna rolled her eyes. Emailing these documents would take too long and would lead to too much of a paper trail.

Heavy footsteps pounded up the stairs.

Anna pointed Joshua to hide under the desk.

"Fucking bastards!" the big boss idiot shouted.

Anna put her transmitting USB into the computer and hid under the desk with Joshua.

She just hoped the big boss idiot didn't find them before the files were transferred.

***

20th July 2022

Southern England, United Kingdom

As much as Joshua loved being this close to sexy beautiful Anna, he was not impressed in the slightest that the big boss idiot was coming for them and he was going to find them.

He didn't even think that Anna could find a way out for them this time. She was extremely smart and just amazing in how she handled herself but this was beyond his skills and surely hers.

The heavy footsteps of the boss pounded into the main office.

Joshua felt his heart rate shoot up. His breathing turned rapid. Sweat poured off him.

Anna gently grabbed his hand and smiled at him. Joshua flat out loved how this amazing person was so confident under pressure and he was really starting to believe that nothing phased her.

"I gonna gun. And I'm gonna use it," the big boss idiot said.

Joshua took large deep breaths and Anna's smile simply grew.

Joshua could see the big boss idiot's large feet under the desk. He was standing centimetres from them.

He walked round the desk.

Joshua couldn't let him hurt Anna. She was too smart, important and clever to die. He had to save her.

Joshua put his feet under him so he could jump out if needed. Anna shook her head.

The big boss idiot stood within striking distance.

Joshua leapt out.

Tackling the idiot to the ground.

Joshua climbed on top of him. Knocking the gun out of his hand.

The idiot whacked Joshua across the room. Pain flooded his jaw. The idiot was strong.

The idiot got up. Charging over to Joshua.

Anna climbed on his back. Slashing his face with her nails.

Joshua ran over to the idiot. Kicking him in the

stomach. He didn't react.

The idiot grabbed Anna. Throwing her against the wall.

The idiot rushed over to Joshua. Punching him.

Joshua collapsed to the ground.

Police sirens echoed outside. The idiot cursed.

Grabbing the gun. Aiming it at Joshua.

Joshua tried to move. He was too battered. Anna tried to stop him. She couldn't move either.

The idiot pressed the barrel against Joshua's head. His fingers tightened around the trigger.

The cops swarmed in. Tackling the idiot to the ground.

Joshua forced himself up and helped Anna up. She kept holding her hips like they were hurting but at least this beautiful woman was alive.

As Joshua left the office, he purposefully tripped near the computer and Anna subtly grabbed the USB transmitter so the police would never find out what they were doing.

And Joshua had a feeling that was exactly how Anna liked it. And Joshua definitely liked her.

***

20th July 2022

Southern England, United Kingdom

A few hours later, Anna sat under a wonderfully cool oak tree with stunning Joshua as they both watched police, environmental agency and other government cars drive into the factory compound.

Anna had made sure to plaster the evidence all

over the internet, and now it was a major news story all over the country as everyone was asking how the hell this sort of thing had happened in the first place. Anna knew it was all down to money and that was what made this pathetic country go round at times.

But at least people were now aware of the corruption and there was even local politicians promising each affected family half a million pounds in compensation, so things were getting done.

And as strange as it sounded to Anna, she honestly believed that the environment was already getting better with the factory getting shut down, and no more toxic chemicals were getting pumped into the river. Amazing hints of pine, fern and crisp fresh air were slowly returning to the local area.

Anna was so happy to see the locals and workers celebrating as the police descended to investigate everything. But most importantly she was just happy to have Joshua by her side, he was so smart, cute and amazing in his own special way.

Anna might have been a professional corporate spy with all the gadgets, knowledge and confidence that the job needed, but it was Joshua that had the balls, boldness and fighting spirit that the job also required.

In all honesty Joshua probably wouldn't have made a bad spy if he was trained correctly and learnt a few things. Anna just smiled at the idea because it was a great idea.

After a good decade of spying alone, unloved and

secretly yearning for some kind of human connection. Anna was excited to finally have it in Joshua and with the money alone from this mission she could live out her days on her horse ranch with her daughter.

She didn't need to keep doing this spy lark, she could just be a mother and Joshua becoming part of their amazing little family if he wanted.

Anna knew she was getting ahead of herself but it was such an amazing dream. But Anna also knew that she loved her job too much. Spying wasn't about the money, it was truly about the justice, adventure and the rush of the job.

She was never going to give it up, or at least not just yet. She would save the money for the horse ranch and still give her daughter the best life she possibly could with the thousands she sent her ex-husband every so often.

But she was a spy first and foremost, and with beautiful Joshua by her side, she could be a great lover.

"What will you do now?" Anna asked as she seductively rested her chin on Joshua's amazingly beautiful shoulders.

He smiled at her and kissed her on the forehead. She loved the sheer power and affection from the kiss.

"I don't know. I've saved my community. My family is basically gone. The future is whatever I make it," he said, giving her an evil smile.

"I could train you if you wanted. I would like you

as a partner and if you really wanted, we could explore whatever *this* is between us," Anna said.

Anna almost felt embarrassed for sounding like such a schoolgirl but it was the truth.

Joshua smiled but bit his lip. "Thought you had a ranch to buy and a daughter to raise,"

"I will in time. My ex-husband treasures our daughter and gives her a normal life. And I love this job too much to give it up yet. So, what do you say? Want to join me and explore whatever relationship we have?"

Joshua kissed her again and again, and Anna seriously loved the passion, love and affection in every single kiss that made her feel like a teenager again.

Within moments Anna had been lovingly pushed onto her back and Anna just knew they were going to go on a lot of missions together, have a lot of fun and definitely explore what their relationship actually was.

But that was all after an afternoon rolling around on the grass together. And Anna couldn't think of a better way to spend a very victorious and wonderful afternoon.

SPY ROMANCE COLLECTION VOLUME 1

A ROMANTIC DROP AT UNIVERSITY
28th September 2022
Canterbury, England

Part-Time MI5 Intelligence Officer Jeremy Clarkes absolutely loved the massive sofa he lowered himself onto with its large red cushions that basically absorbed his small body, the very comfortable black fabric that was slightly cold to the touch that wrapped around his lower region and he really enjoy the peace and quiet of the wide long wooden hallway he was in.

The hallway itself probably wasn't anything too special to the university students that came here each and every day, and Jeremy supposed when he had been a student here at Kent University, this long and very wide corridor with its smooth wooden walls to the left, a few wooden doors that led into grand music halls and on the right there were massive floor-to-ceiling windows, he hadn't cared either.

Maybe the so-called grand designer of the university believed the floor-to-ceiling windows were meant to be nice, beautiful or impressive. But in reality it was a minor shame that the windows only looked out onto a narrow concrete path between this building and another grey university building that Jeremy believed was the biology building.

But Jeremy was hardly going to hold the sheer lack of view against the designer, because the wide, long wooden corridor was rather nice and Jeremy was more than happy to wait here until his contact came to meet him.

The air smelt wonderful with great thick aromas of bitter coffee, sweet creamy cakes and even the amazing smell of juicy crispy bacon came from the little university restaurant at the far end of the corridor past some stairs, groups of students and the half-broken wooden door to another lecture theatre.

The great sound of students talking, laughing and debating how unfair their coursework was this term just made Jeremy smile, because he had been out of university for a few years now after studying psychology (which wasn't profiling like every single person believed that really did annoy Jeremy) and he was working part-time on his Master degree whilst helping out MI5 at the same time.

Jeremy really loved how his dad had wanted him to work for MI5 and work for his department, but Jeremy had really wanted to get his Masters in clinical psychology (or mental health as Jeremy explained to everyone else) so instead Jeremy's dad *bullied* (more like pleaded) for Jeremy to work part time for MI5.

So Jeremy agreed.

Granted Jeremy never believed he would have to return to his old university to meet a contact that meant to be giving him a memory stick containing information. Since apparently MI5 believed one of the professors at the University was meant to be selling secrets to the Russians because Kent University had a number of top-secret government contracts.

Jeremy had to admit his old university was impressive as hell because they had managed to get government contracts on a range of issues, like cybersecurity, research new materials for body armour and even highly advanced communications systems.

It was great that Kent University was doing this sort of work but Jeremy was a little concerned that there was a possible enemy operative in the university.

Ideally Jeremy would have liked his dad to give him the mission of *deposing* of the threat to national security but apparently his dad didn't believe he was ready for that sort of responsibility.

Jeremy completely disagreed, because Jeremy had slept with enemy agents to get classified Brazilian, French and Spanish intelligence and he had even had to kill a few of them by *accident*, so Jeremy just couldn't understand why he wasn't allowed to end this threat to national security.

The beautiful sound of two men laughing as they walked past made Jeremy smile a little, and Jeremy had to admit they really did look beautiful in their dark blue jeans, blue jumpers and smooth round faces.

Jeremy had seriously missed the university scene for young men, and university had actually been an amazing time for him. He had first learnt he was gay here, he had lost his virginity and he had really learnt the sort of person who he wanted to be.

Granted no one here would have been able to tell he was gay or even an intelligence officer, because he had really tried for the student-look today, or at least what he called the student-look. Some tight sexy blue jeans, a white t-shirt that showed how slim he was and some black trainers.

It might not have been as attractive as the sporty men walking around university with their sportswear, but Jeremy knew he looked pretty cute, and judging by the range of looks he had gotten earlier from men and women he sort of knew that he was completely right.

Jeremy checked the time on his black smartphone and it was coming up to midday, and Jeremy just really hoped that the contact he was meeting would show up soon.

He still had a lot of reading to do for his Masters degree after this meeting and after he had travelled to see his dad to hand over the memory stick.

Jeremy just really hoped that the contact wouldn't be too long because the longer MI5 didn't have that memory stick, the longer that foul rogue professor was out on the streets selling information to the Russians.

And Jeremy just knew from personal experience how deadly that really was.

**

28th September 2022
Canterbury, England

PhD Student William Conner leant against the slightly cold red brick wall of a very large and very long glass building that housed the university's libraries with tens of thousands of books and several cafes and workstations for students where William studied. He really liked the slight coldness that radiated through his white shirt, chequered blue trousers and his brown shoes.

He just felt like he needed the coldness more than anything today, and he really wasn't sure if he was doing the right thing.

William just focused on the constantly moving sea of students in all their different heights, weights and ethnic origins flow up and down the brick path ahead of him. He didn't recognise any of them at all but that was hardly surprising considering it was the first week back at university for everyone, so there were thousands of new students that had just joined.

But at least there were some cute boys that William didn't recognise. There was one very cute boy that might have been 22 or 23, just a year or two younger than himself, with longish brown hair and a perfectly round face that was walking towards the library.

The crisp, refreshing and slightly damp air surrounded William as he felt a little excited for a moment until the cute boy smiled and kissed his girlfriend, and William just laughed a little.

All the students were talking to each other, catching up on their summers, what they wanted out of this year and what they thought of their courses so far. It was so amazing to hear so many voices again and it really was like the university campus was finally back to normal after the eerie silence of the summer months.

But William just realised he must have been kidding himself if he seriously believed that dating would actually be any easier this year. He was 24 years old, bisexual and he had barely been able to do too much dating in recent years.

He seriously loved women but after dating a few last years and in his Masters and Undergraduate degrees, he just wanted to try dating a man. He had only dated one seriously hot guy in High school but that had ended awfully.

Yet the problem was always the same for all gay or bisexual people, William just had absolutely no clue how the hell he was going to meet a hot cute man to fall in love with. It was seriously the bane of his life, and he had wondered about going to the university's LGBT+ society on Friday but that just didn't seem like his sort of thing.

He tried to just forget about his dating problems as he looked at the time on his large blue smartphone and it was starting to approach midday. He still couldn't believe that he was actually meant to be meeting a spy or Intelligence Officer as they preferred to be called to hand over a memory stick.

William still felt so guilty about it all, and he really didn't want to do it, because Professor Davenport had seriously been so great to William, without Davenport William really doubted he would have gotten onto the PhD position (because of department politics for than anything else) and the professor had been a great supervisor.

It just seemed so wrong of William to hand over the memory stick and all the information that could get the professor arrested or even worse, killed.

But William had to hand over the stupid memory stick more than anything else in the world, his father had been murdered by Russia-backed insurrectionists in Afghanistan so William was not allowing the damn pathetic Russians to hurt him anymore.

And if the price to protect the UK, like his father would have wanted, was to make a "good" man go to prison then that was okay to William. It just had to be okay.

William took a deep breath of the crisp, refreshing air and took a few steps forward and merged with the endless stream of the students going in and out of the library and past it.

William just kept following the brick path ahead of him, trying not to knock into the other students as he hooked a left onto another brick path towards the university building he was meant to be meeting the Intelligence Officer in.

He didn't even know what the officer looked like, he didn't know if he was expecting James Bond, a man in a suit or street clothes or anything. William was completely in the dark, and part of him just wanted the man or woman to be hot.

That wouldn't be a problem.

But William forced himself not to get his hopes up as most intelligence officers were probably older men and women in their 30s or older. A little out of William's age range but he seriously wished the officer would be hot.

And just because he had read a few spy novels last night (something he fully admitted he should not have done because the informant always dies in them) and learnt that a lot of contacts get pickpocketed before dying, William placed his hands in his jean pockets.

Thankfully the small black memory stick was still in there so William simply wrapped his fingers around it.

After a few more moments of walking along the long brick path and got to a very modern-looking wooden university building, William went through some glass doors, hooked a right and went down a very wide and long corridor with massive sofas and smooth wooden walls to his left and horrible floor-to-ceiling windows to his right.

William really didn't like the windows because

they were so awful, tasteless and the designer had to be an idiot because of the sheer lack of view and-

William stopped dead in his tracks as he looked at the most beautiful man he had ever seen sitting on one of the large black sofas in the corridor.

The man was so hot and beautiful and sexy with his white t-shirt that showed how seriously fit he was, his tight blue jeans that only amplified his raw sexual appeal even more and William really, really loved the man's cute little square face that looked so young and innocent but there was just something about his eyes.

Maybe other students here looked at the hot sexy man and presumed he was another student that was innocent in the ways of the world, but William just recognised something.

A certain type of emotional damage or experience behind the hot man's sexy emerald eyes that made William instantly know that the beautiful man was the intelligence officer he was meant to be meeting.

And William couldn't help but realise the hot man was a little young, maybe only a year younger than him, William had absolutely no problem with hopefully getting to know this sexy, hot, beautiful man a little better.

And that all came with the hopeful bonus of helping to protect the UK as well.

***

28th September 2022
Canterbury, England

As much as Jeremy loved the amazing softness of the large black sofa with its pillows and wonderful fabric, Jeremy was seriously starting to wonder if this contact would ever show up, and even worse what if the entire mission had been compromised?

That had already happened to Jeremy far more times than he actually wanted to think about. The last time in Paris with the French DGSE, the Italian Mob and a scared cute man was not Jeremy's idea of fun in the slightest, so Jeremy just really hoped that the mission was fine.

As it was lunchtime, the sound of students talking, moving and catching up on their summers got louder and louder as more students came into the university building and dived into the restaurant at the far end of the corridor, but they were all so loud that the sound carried perfectly.

Jeremy was about to move further up the wooden corridor to another large black sofa when he noticed someone coming towards him. He couldn't see who it was exactly because they were sort of merged into the endless stream of students coming into the corridor.

If this person had intelligence training then Jeremy had to admit they were excellent, because they would be far too close to Jeremy for comfort before he had properly assessed if they were a threat or not.

But then he actually saw the guy.

The second the hot sexy guy stepped into perfect view Jeremy was just shocked to the core.

He had absolutely no idea how the hot sexy guy could look so average and rather unappealing in the few photos and pieces of paper that his father had given him, but in reality the guy actually looked like a god.

Jeremy seriously loved the guy's amazing looking legs in his jeans, the crisp white shirt that made him look so intelligent, clever and sexy with the wonderful added bonus of it showing how slim the guy was underneath.

And Jeremy seriously loved how cute the guy was with his longish fluffy brown hair that he really, really wanted to run his fingers through, his slight brown beard and Jeremy just knew the guy's smooth, youthful face was simply adorable.

The guy was sheer perfection and probably one of the most beautiful guys Jeremy had actually ever seen, and that included a lot of foreign agents trying to attack the UK.

Jeremy felt his hands turn sweaty and he felt sweat slowly roll down his back and his wayward parts flare to life as he stared at the sexy hunk of a guy that was walking towards him.

Then the hot sexy guy simply came over to him and held out the little black memory stick that contained all the information to save or damn the UK.

The hot sexy guy didn't ask if Jeremy was the Officer he was meant to meet, he didn't know if Jeremy was friendly and Jeremy was just shocked at him.

If he had been anyone else in the slightest, Jeremy would have been mad, a little annoyed and so infuriated that a person with no intelligence training could have destroyed UK national security by making such a simple mistake.

Jeremy just couldn't believe this hot sexy guy had been willing to hand over the memory stick so easily. What if Jeremy had been working for the professor or the Russians?

But as much as Jeremy wanted to be annoyed with this very cute fool, he actually couldn't bring himself to be any of that. All he could do was simply stare into the beautifully soft brown eyes of this guy and really want to know more about him.

Yet he had a job to do first.

Jeremy gently smiled and shook his head as he took the memory stick of the guy, making sure their fingers grazed each other for a moment. And Jeremy seriously loved the smoothness and tenderness of the guy's warm, slightly sweaty, skin against his own.

And Jeremy could have sworn he felt the beautiful guy's fingers stretch out a little more as if they both never wanted this moment to end and they both wanted to hold each other's hands for a little longer.

Jeremy really wanted that, more than anything else in the entire world at the moment actually, but he sadly forced himself to pull away and took out his black smartphone.

One of the same benefits of working for MI5 was that Jeremy got access to a lot of great apps that he really loved, including a smartphone app that allowed him to scan memory sticks without them having to be plugged in. He had absolutely no idea how it worked but it was an amazing app for sure.

"What's that?" the guy asked.

Jeremy smiled at him and he felt his smile turn into a sexy grin as he looked at the amazing guy in front of him.

When he had met informants or contacts before, they were normally so scared, concerned or nervous, but this guy wasn't. That could have meant that the guy had no idea what he was actually involved in, but as he was doing a PhD Jeremy really doubted he was that stupid.

Or this amazing guy was clearly curious and Jeremy really liked that in a guy.

Jeremy gestured for both of them to sit down on the large black sofa and the guy slowly nodded and they both did.

Jeremy was fairly sure that if he looked at any MI5 policy or rulebook, he wasn't meant to sit back down once he had the asset (the memory stick) in case they were attacked and technically his mission now was to validate the memory stick was real and get it as soon as possible to MI5.

But around this really hot sexy guy, Jeremy just didn't want to leave yet and he even wanted to get to know this beautiful guy a little more.

"Can I know you're name?" the hot sexy guy asked.

Jeremy smiled. He said it so nervously and with such a schoolboy grin that the guy looked so cute and Jeremy was slightly willing to bend a rule or two for this cutie.

"Only my first name but I'm Jeremy," he said holding out his hand.

The guy unleashed another sexy schoolboy grin that melted Jeremy's heart but Jeremy hated it when he had to take back his hand before the guy shook it because his phone buzzed.

"I'm William," the hot guy said.

"Hot name," Jeremy said, regretting it the moment he said it. "Um, sorry I'm normally more professional than this,"

Jeremy really couldn't believe he had actually just said that to a contact, he hated being so unprofessional but this guy was just so cute.

Then it hit Jeremy that he really needed to make himself not like this guy. MI5 Officers couldn't fall for contacts or anything, it was the rules and this guy was a PhD student and he was only a Masters student.

They weren't exactly compatible.

Jeremy forced his attention back to his phone and smiled that the memory stick did actually contain all the information MI5 needed.

"Wow," Jeremy said as he scrolled through some of the data. "This is amazing. This contains email addresses, bank accounts and details every little document the professor sent,"

Jeremy just looked at sexy William and smiled. He had met some good and great contacts before during his part-time intelligence work but William might be the best. He had never seen information this detailed before, it was perfect.

Just like William so far.

"Thank you," Jeremy said. "This is amazing,"

William shrugged like it was nothing but Jeremy saw in his eyes that he was conflicted.

And as much as Jeremy just needed to leave and get the memory stick to MI5 he made himself stay a little longer.

"Can I ask your age?" William asked.

Jeremy's raised his eyebrows a little, it was nothing that he hadn't heard before.

"Sorry, sorry," William said. "I'm not normally like a teenager. I'm normally quite intelligent and know exactly what to say it's just I haven't met someone like you before,"

If anyone else had said that Jeremy might have taken it as William not meeting an intelligence officer before but he seriously hoped it was that William found him attractive.

Because Jeremy really wasn't sure what he would do if William didn't like him, because Jeremy was just wanting to get to know this amazingly hot guy more and more with each passing second.

"I do this part-time," Jeremy said wanting to be as truthful as he could with hot sexy William but being careful at the same time. "I'm a psychology Masters student by day,"

It was great to see William's eyes light up.

"Then we can all talk," someone said.

Jeremy looked up away from the black sofa for a moment and just frowned as he saw three men standing there.

Jeremy would have known the middle-aged man standing in the middle from anywhere. He had stared the professor Davenport's face too many times from surveillance footage and personnel records for Jeremy not to know what he looked like.

But Davenport seriously didn't know how to dress well. The professor was wearing a very worn and ancient grey trench coat from the 1950s, his bald head looked awful and his rough skin really didn't help the look.

Yet Jeremy was a little more concerned about the two slightly younger men with their classic Russian looks, short blond hair and strong jawlines. They were rather attractive in a way but judging how they were holding their black overcoats Jeremy sort of knew they were holding guns under them.

Not what Jeremy wanted.

If MI5 found out about this little problem then Jeremy just knew they would moan at him because he should have left already and now because of his feelings for a very hot guy he risked losing the memory stick.

But Jeremy couldn't help as his stomach twisted

into a painful knot as he realised that he didn't only risk losing the memory stick but he also risked losing William.

It was so stupid to be worrying about losing a hot guy he had only just met but Jeremy really felt drawn to him and he was quickly realising he was rather desperate for a first date or something with this hottie.

As professor Davenport took a step closer Jeremy just knew without a shadow of a doubt he had a lot to do. He had to save the UK from the Russians, protect the memory stick and most importantly save the really attractive man sitting right next to him.

Jeremy just had to do all of those things or die trying.

***

28th September 2022

Canterbury, England

William just flat couldn't believe this was happening. Sure he had been nervous and concerned that Professor Davenport and his crazy Russian friends might show up and try to stop him but for it to actually happen was something else entirely.

William felt his heart pound in his chest and he was fairly certain that something very, very bad was going to happen to them all as they all stood there staring at each other in the wide, long wooden corridor.

"Let's go to my office men," Professor Davenport said as a group of female university students walked past.

William was actually about to take a step forward like Davenport and his two Russian friends were the ones in complete control but he was rather amazed that beautiful Jeremy simply sat back down.

William had to admit Jeremy was so beautiful and cute as he sat down on the large black sofa and simply allowed the massive black cushions to swallow his body whole. Jeremy was seriously cute and William really wanted to protect him.

But given how Jeremy was the professional spy, William just sort of wanted to follow his lead.

So he sat down to next to Jeremy. He was probably sitting far too close to Jeremy for comfort but given how beautiful Jeremy was William actually wanted to be even closer to him.

Davenport laughed. "Wow. William I gave you everything, I allowed you get onto the PhD programme, I supported you and I kept supporting you. And this is how you repay me?"

William looked to the floor as Davenport's words slammed into him. The sad truth was that Davenport was actually right, he really had done so much for William whenever no one else would and he was basically betraying him.

Then Jeremy handed a perfectly warm hand over William's and William's pounding heart skipped a few beats.

"You know he's only manipulating you," Davenport said. "It's what they do and you are such an easy mark,"

William glanced at Jeremy slightly and he really didn't want to believe that everything Jeremy had said in those few precious sentences between them was a lie.

He really wanted to believe that Jeremy cared about him, was attracted to him and seriously wanted to get to know him better. But what if it was all a lie and a simple spy trick?

What if Davenport was simply doing the same?

The two Russians said something loud in Russian and whipped out their guns and aimed them at William and Jeremy.

William was about to lean protectively over Jeremy but Jeremy beat him too.

Jeremy smelt amazing with his hints of his earthy aftershave but now really wasn't the time. William had to help Jeremy get them out of this situation.

The other students sitting on the other sofas screamed and shouted and ran.

William wanted to panic but Jeremy was almost projecting a very hot aura of calm that William just couldn't help but relax.

"Give me the memory stick," Davenport said. "Or believe me my friends will kill you both,"

William smiled. "Impossible. Your friends aren't your friends. They're your Masters and we all know the armed police would be coming right now,"

As William watched Davenport and the Russians tense, he found it so weird that Jeremy tensed as well.

The Russians raised their guns. They fired.

The massive floor-to-ceiling window behind William shattered.

"Give the stick," the Russians said.

Jeremy stood up. William did the same.

Jeremy took the memory stick out of his pocket. William felt his stomach twist. This couldn't be happening.

William hated it how Jeremy was about to hand over the memory stick.

Davenport took a few steps closer.

William leant forward.

Davenport's eyes widened.

The Russians surged forward.

Punching William in the stomach. Putting him into a headlock.

William hated the Russian's rough overcoat and his captor tightened the headlock.

He hated seeing Jeremy upset even more. William felt awful as Jeremy looked so disappointed, sad and like he had just failed.

"I was going to do the same to Davenport," Jeremy said.

William gave Jeremy a weak smile and even though he could sort of guess that Jeremy was a bit annoyed Jeremy still looked so cute.

The other Russian pressed the cold metal barrel of his gun against the bottom of William's jaw and looked at Jeremy.

"The memory stick now or I will paint the walls

with his brains," he said.

Jeremy swallowed hard and William could only begin to imagine how hard this was for him.

Jeremy was basically going to be risking his entire country just for the sake of William. He really hated himself at that, William just wished that he was better.

But he was a PhD student as Davenport had said. Maybe he could figure out a way to save them all.

Jeremy held out the little black memory stick towards Davenport.

"You know that won't help," William said.

William hated it how the Russian headlock-ing him tightened his grip.

"Why?" Davenport said.

"Because MI5 already has the information. He scanned it earlier," William said.

"Stupid idiot," the Russian holding the gun to William said.

The same Russian took the gun away from William and shot Davenport in the back of the head.

Davenport's corpse slumped to the ground.

William really didn't like this anymore. Even Jeremy looked shocked or at least surprised.

The Russian with the gun pointed it at Jeremy's head.

"Sorry about this we need to cover up all loose ends now," he said.

William couldn't have this. He couldn't have Jeremy dying. He was too beautiful and William had to go out on a date with him.

William jumped up. His neck ached.

He slammed his feet into the Russian holding him.

The Russian hissed.

His grip weakened.

William slammed his elbow into his ribs.

The Russian with the guy looked at William.

Jeremy flew forward.

Tackling the Russian with the gun to the ground.

William headbutted the Russian holding him.

The Russian released him.

William spun around.

Punching the man in the nose.

Kicking him in-between the legs.

The Russian fell to the ground.

William jumped on him.

Some ribs broke.

William was just about to knock the man down when armed police officers in black body armour and face masks stormed in.

William spun around to make sure beautiful Jeremy was okay but he was gone.

And William honestly expected himself to be mad, sad or concerned that such a beautiful man had disappeared on him but he actually wasn't. Jeremy was a beautiful, hot man that he really, really liked but he was a part-time spy and even William knew deep down that surely a relationship between a PhD student and a spy could never ever work.

But it would have been nice to try and William seriously wondered where the hell Jeremy had gone to?

***

28th September 2022

Canterbury, England

A few hours later, William had finally finished giving his statement to the armed police officers at the university and suffered through even more interrogations with people in black suits after he stupidly mentioned the involvement of MI5, Russians and a memory stick. But now it was finally over William was so looking forward to going home at last.

William went into one of Kent University's many massive square concrete car parks that had rows upon rows of little car park spaces with large thick oak trees lining the edges. It wasn't the most attractive of car parks with the ugly grey brick university buildings slightly beyond the oak trees but it was a great car park.

And as the sky turned a fiery orange as the sun started to set, William was a little disappointed that he had spent so much of the afternoon and early evening talking to police officers, men in black suit and all whilst pining over a man he barely knew.

As William slowly walked past a lot of empty car park spaces because everyone else had already gone home, and the slight warmth from the perfectly smooth concrete gently pulsed through his shoes and into his feet, William was really surprised at the sort of impression that Jeremy had left on him.

William had been so cute, beautiful and hot so William just sort of supposed that it was normal for him to like Jeremy because he had also been searching for a hot man to date for ages, but he just felt like it was more than that.

Not only because Jeremy was a part-time spy (which was always a very attractive job) but he was clever, kind and he was a psychology student himself. William liked to believe that all he really wanted was a beautiful kind man that would love him, and he could love too and with them both being psychology students that would give him a lot to talk about.

And it would hopefully be a good foundation to build a relationship on.

As William got deeper into the massive square car park, William could see his little blue Ford Fiesta and to his utter surprise there was a very cute man leaning against it. Sure the man was wearing a baseball cap and completely different clothes to earlier but William instantly recognised it as Jeremy.

Why was he here?

William quickly walked over to him.

William had to admit Jeremy did look amazing in his slightly baggier black jeans, black shirt and boots that didn't really highlight anything about him but William wouldn't have been surprised if it helped him to blend into places where he didn't want to be seen.

But William really didn't care at that moment, not only because he had thankfully seen Jeremy in something extremely attractive earlier but because his beautiful Jeremy was here for him.

And that seriously meant everything to him.

Jeremy waved and smiled at William and Jeremy's sensational smile just melted his heart again, and there was such warmth behind it too.

William realised that Davenport had been completely wrong in his own manipulation, Jeremy didn't hold his hand to manipulate William, he had held his hand because Jeremy really wanted him.

Just like why Jeremy was here now instead of doing whatever for his own degree or MI5 job.

He wanted William and William really, really wanted him.

"I didn't expect to see you again," William said, slowly going over to Jeremy and he didn't even care that he was probably getting a little too close to Jeremy.

William only stopped when he accidentally realised that he was so close to beautiful Jeremy that he could feel Jeremy's amazing wonderful body heat against him.

Jeremy only smiled. "My bosses didn't either but it turns out, and this is all only hypothetical of course, but the Ministry of Defence is offering your university a lot more contracts and China, Russian and our other enemies are... excited about this,"

William smiled, he just hoped this was going where he seriously hoped it was.

"So I have managed to persuade my bosses and

university to let me transfer here," Jeremy said.

William just grinned like a little silly schoolboy as Jeremy took another step closer to him. So close that William could feel Jeremy's wonderfully sweet-scented breath on his neck.

William so badly wanted to kiss Jeremy at that moment.

"I was wondering if you were okay with that and if you, you know, wanted to get to know each other a little bit?" Jeremy asked looking at the floor with his own very cute schoolboy smile.

William couldn't believe how cute Jeremy looked even when he looked so embarrassed and shy. William couldn't actually believe Jeremy thought he was going to reject him.

William would have loved nothing else.

But what if he wasn't the right sort of man with a spy? Even a part-time one. Would Jeremy be constantly concerned about William's safety so he would take his eye off the ball and risk his own safety.

William didn't want Jeremy to be constantly worrying about him, and William didn't want Jeremy to be constantly stressed and if the UK's enemies were really concerning the university as much as Jeremy believed then surely William shouldn't bother Jeremy with a relationship. Did he have more important things to focus on than him?

"And," Jeremy said kissing William on the cheek that made William gasp with pleasure. "My father was wondering if you would like to come into the fold.

You got us the information from Davenport, I said you were great when confronted with the Russians and I… I would really like to see you more,"

William smiled a little more and his own face started to hurt as he realised what exactly Jeremy was asking him to do. And it did actually make perfect sense, who the hell would ever suspect a PhD student as a spy or *intelligence Officer* as he was probably going to have to start calling himself.

"Please?" Jeremy asked. "Will you do it?"

If it was anything else in the entire world, William was fairly sure he would have said no because he was a bisexual man that loved his sexuality, being a psychology PhD student and he loved his quiet non-spying life. But for some reason he simply kissed Jeremy on the lips.

He loved the silky smoothness of Jeremy's warm lips against his own and he simply nodded.

He actually enjoyed stealing information from Professor Davenport a lot more than he realised and as William unlocked his car and Jeremy got in with him, he really excited for the future.

Because it didn't actually matter what happened now, because William was going to become an *Intelligence Officer* and spend a lot of amazing time with beautiful Jeremy and if things didn't work out then that was okay.

Jeremy had already given him a lot of great gifts, William finally knew that he could find hot attractive men, he could finally become a spy and continue his father's work about protecting the UK and he had finally felt the start of *love* or utterly great attraction towards Jeremy.

But William and Jeremy both got in the car, and William just looked at how cute, beautiful and wonderful Jeremy looked sitting next to him, he seriously just knew that Jeremy was the one.

And he was seriously looking forward to getting to know Jeremy a lot, lot more but for now at least William just kissed him.

Again and again.

***

16th June 2023

Canterbury, England

An entire academic year later, Jeremy and William sat on Kent University's massive bright green field that looked out over the wonderful historical city of Canterbury with its ancient high street, impressive cathedral and tall spires in the distance. Jeremy really loved it how he had just finished his last exam of the year and William was resting his sexy little face on his lap as they both sat (or laid in William's case) on the grass.

It was a perfectly warm day, the sun was high in the sky and there was even an amazingly cool breeze with hints of pine, freshness and candy floss from a stall tens of metres away on the main university campus.

Jeremy gently ran his fingers through William's wonderfully fluffy hair and he was so pleased, happy and excited for what had happened over the past academic year.

Jeremy had worked a lot of MI5 cases part-time, meeting contacts and doing other work, but this was the first year that he could actually say without lying that this was a fun job. And it was only now that he realised that all the other times he had said it was *fun*, he had been lying.

He hadn't even known how great his part-time job was until he worked with William. William was still training in intelligence work and he really did bring such flare, style and sense of fun to the seriousness of a very deadly job.

Together they had found out what "students" were actually foreign agents, they had stopped top-secret military experiments being sent to hostile powers and Jeremy's favourite task was whenever the two of them had to make out to stop them from getting caught.

Because Jeremy was seriously glad that English and foreign agents and people had a massive aversion to walking into the same room as two guys making out. And it also helped that William really was an amazing kisser too.

So as the cooling breeze picked up a little, Jeremy just stared at the stunning fluffy hunk of a man who's head was on his lap, and Jeremy just bend down and kissed him.

Really passionately.

And Jeremy was expecting William to question or

ask what that was for, but he didn't, and that really summed it up for Jeremy.

The problem with being an intelligence officer that had relationships were they were often needy, chaotic and hard to prioritise over the work, yet William wasn't like that at all. He was so easy to work with, love with and just be with that Jeremy really, really knew that they were perfect for each other.

Sure Jeremy was joining Kent University's PhD programme, the same one as William, next year so they could both become doctors, work in the university and still do their job for MI5, but they weren't scared about it.

All because their relationship was so strong, perfect and they loved each other so much that they were actually really looking forward to it both.

And as Jeremy kissed William again and again, he knew that they were perfect for each other and this wasn't some fling between two guys. This was real, special and something that was going to last for a very, very long time indeed.

And that was exactly how Jeremy wanted it and judging by how hard and passionately William was kissing him back, he seriously didn't mind either.

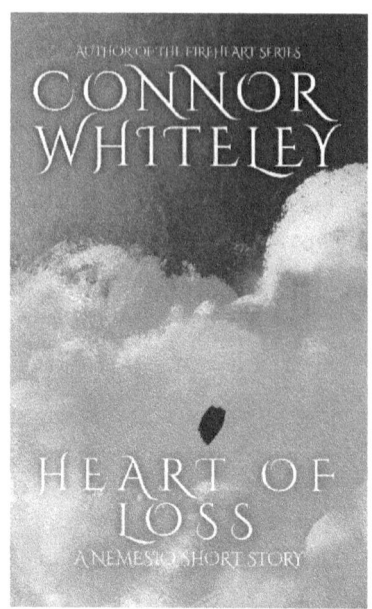

GET YOUR FREE AND EXCLUSIVE SHORT STORY NOW! LEARN ABOUT NEMESIO'S PAST!

https://www.subscribepage.com/fireheart

Keep up to date with exclusive deals on Connor Whiteley's Books, as well as the latest news about new releases and so much more!

Sign up for the Grab a Book and Chill Monthly newsletter, and you'll get one **FREE** ebook just for signing up: Agents of The Emperor Collection.

Sign Up Now!

https://dl.bookfunnel.com/f4p5xkprbk

About the author:

Connor Whiteley is the author of over 60 books in the sci-fi fantasy, nonfiction psychology and books for writer's genre and he is a Human Branding Speaker and Consultant.

He is a passionate warhammer 40,000 reader, psychology student and author.

Who narrates his own audiobooks and he hosts The Psychology World Podcast.

All whilst studying Psychology at the University of Kent, England.

Also, he was a former Explorer Scout where he gave a speech to the Maltese President in August 2018 and he attended Prince Charles' 70th Birthday Party at Buckingham Palace in May 2018.

Plus, he is a self-confessed coffee lover!

OTHER SHORT STORIES BY CONNOR WHITELEY

Mystery Short Stories:
Protecting The Woman She Hated
Finding A Royal Friend
Our Woman In Paris
Corrupt Driving
A Prime Assassination
Jubilee Thief
Jubilee, Terror, Celebrations
Negative Jubilation
Ghostly Jubilation
Killing For Womenkind
A Snowy Death
Miracle Of Death
A Spy In Rome
The 12:30 To St Pancreas
A Country In Trouble
A Smokey Way To Go
A Spicy Way To GO
A Marketing Way To Go
A Missing Way To Go
A Showering Way To Go
Poison In The Candy Cane
Christmas Innocence
You Better Watch Out
Christmas Theft
Trouble In Christmas
Smell of The Lake
Problem In A Car

SPY ROMANCE COLLECTION VOLUME 1

Theft, Past and Team
Embezzler In The Room
A Strange Way To Go
A Horrible Way To Go
Ann Awful Way To Go
An Old Way To Go
A Fishy Way To Go
A Pointy Way To Go
A High Way To Go
A Fiery Way To Go
A Glassy Way To Go
A Chocolatey Way To Go
Kendra Detective Mystery Collection Volume 1
Kendra Detective Mystery Collection Volume 2
Stealing A Chance At Freedom
Glassblowing and Death
Theft of Independence
Cookie Thief
Marble Thief
Book Thief
Art Thief
Mated At The Morgue
The Big Five Whoopee Moments
Stealing An Election
Mystery Short Story Collection Volume 1
Mystery Short Story Collection Volume 2
Criminal Performance
Candy Detectives
Key To Birth In The Past

<u>Science Fiction Short Stories:</u>
Temptation
Superhuman Autospy
Blood In The Redwater
All Is Dust
Vigil
Emperor Forgive Us
Their Brave New World
Gummy Bear Detective
The Candy Detective
What Candies Fear
The Blurred Image
Shattered Legions
The First Rememberer
Life of A Rememberer
System of Wonder
Lifesaver
Remarkable Way She Died
The Interrogation of Annabella Stormic
Blade of The Emperor
Arbiter's Truth
Computation of Battle
Old One's Wrath
Puppets and Masters
Ship of Plague
Interrogation
Edge of Failure
One Way Choice
Acceptable Losses
Balance of Power

SPY ROMANCE COLLECTION VOLUME 1

Good Idea At The Time
Escape Plan
Escape In The Hesitation
Inspiration In Need
Singing Warriors
Knowledge is Power
Killer of Polluters
Climate of Death
The Family Mailing Affair
Defining Criminality
The Martian Affair
A Cheating Affair
The Little Café Affair
Mountain of Death
Prisoner's Fight
Claws of Death
Bitter Air
Honey Hunt
Blade On A Train
<u>Fantasy Short Stories:</u>
City of Snow
City of Light
City of Vengeance
Dragons, Goats and Kingdom
Smog The Pathetic Dragon
Don't Go In The Shed
The Tomato Saver
The Remarkable Way She Died
The Bloodied Rose
Asmodia's Wrath

Heart of A Killer
Emissary of Blood
Dragon Coins
Dragon Tea
Dragon Rider
Sacrifice of the Soul
Heart of The Flesheater
Heart of The Regent
Heart of The Standing
Feline of The Lost
Heart of The Story
City of Fire
Awaiting Death

Other books by Connor Whiteley:
Bettie English Private Eye Series
A Very Private Woman
The Russian Case
A Very Urgent Matter
A Case Most Personal
Trains, Scots and Private Eyes
The Federation Protects

Lord of War Origin Trilogy:
Not Scared Of The Dark
Madness
Burn It All

The Fireheart Fantasy Series
Heart of Fire
Heart of Lies
Heart of Prophecy
Heart of Bones
Heart of Fate

City of Assassins (Urban Fantasy)
City of Death
City of Marytrs
City of Pleasure
City of Power

Agents of The Emperor
Return of The Ancient Ones
Vigilance
Angels of Fire
Kingmaker
The Eight
The Lost Generation

Lord Of War Trilogy (Agents of The Emperor)
Not Scared Of The Dark
Madness
Burn It All Down

The Garro Series- Fantasy/Sci-fi
GARRO: GALAXY'S END
GARRO: RISE OF THE ORDER
GARRO: END TIMES
GARRO: SHORT STORIES

GARRO: COLLECTION
GARRO: HERESY
GARRO: FAITHLESS
GARRO: DESTROYER OF WORLDS
GARRO: COLLECTIONS BOOK 4-6
GARRO: MISTRESS OF BLOOD
GARRO: BEACON OF HOPE
GARRO: END OF DAYS

Winter Series- Fantasy Trilogy Books
WINTER'S COMING
WINTER'S HUNT
WINTER'S REVENGE
WINTER'S DISSENSION

Miscellaneous:
RETURN
FREEDOM
SALVATION
Reflection of Mount Flame
The Masked One
The Great Deer

Gay Romance Novellas
Breaking, Nursing, Repairing A Broken Heart
Jacob And Daniel
Fallen For A Lie
His Heartstopper
Spying And Weddings

www.ingramcontent.com/pod-product-compliance
Lightning Source LLC
LaVergne TN
LVHW012112070526
838202LV00056B/5701